Barnabe Googe, Edward Arber

Eglogs, Epythapes & Sonettes

Anatiposi

Barnabe Googe, Edward Arber

Eglogs, Epythapes & Sonettes

Reprint of the original, first published in 1871.

1st Edition 2023 | ISBN: 978-3-38212-661-2

Anatiposi Verlag is an imprint of Outlook Verlagsgesellschaft mbH.

Verlag (Publisher): Outlook Verlag GmbH, Zeilweg 44, 60439 Frankfurt, Deutschland
Vertretungsberechtigt (Authorized to represent): E. Roepke, Zeilweg 44, 60439 Frankfurt, Deutschland
Druck (Print): Books on Demand GmbH, In de Tarpen 42, 22848 Norderstedt, Deutschland

English Reprints.

BARNABE GOOGE.

Eglogs, Epytaphes, & Sonettes.

1563.

THREE COPIES ONLY AT PRESENT KNOWN.

FROM THE COPY IN THE POSSESSION OF HENRY HUTH, ESQRE.

CAREFULLY EDITED BY

EDWARD ARBER,

Associate, King's College, London, A.K.C., F.R.G.S., &c.

LONDON:

5 QUEEN SQUARE, BLOOMSBURY, W.C.

Ent. Stat. Hall.] 1 December 1871.

CONTENTS.

By Barnabe Googe.

ECLOGUES.

EPITAPHS.

SONNETS, &c.

CUPIDO CONQUERED.

L. Blundeston.

Alexander Neville.

NOTES of the LIFE and WRITINGS of BARNABE GOOGE.

His furname is alfo varioufly fpelt *Goche*, *Goghe*, *Gouche*, &c.

There was printed at Venice an undated Latin satirical poem in twelve books named after the signs of the Zodiac. *Zodiacus*
[? **1535–1539**] *Vitæ pulcherrimmo opus atque utilissimum, Marcelli Palingenii stellati Poetæ ad illustrissimum Ferrariæ Ducem Hercules secundem feliciter incipit.* The dedication to Hercules II. d'Este, who was Duke of Ferrara between 1 Nov. 1534–3 Oct. 1559, fixes the date of the impression, to which Thomas Scauranus prefaced a few verses. Marcellus Palingenius is believed to be an anagram for Pietro Angelo Manzolli, an Italian, respecting whose life very little is known. We have printed Googe's own account of him at p. 13. Despite its being put on the Index by the Council of Trent; more than twenty editions of this celebrated Invective have been published in Latin and other languages; including two Latin editions at Basle in 1552 and 1557, which Googe may have used in his translation and another at London in 1579.

1553. FEB. 20. Thomas Kirchmeyer or Naogeorgus [*b.* 1511–*d.* 29 Dec. 1563] was the author of another anti-Papist invective in verse, entitled *Regni Papistici*, the preface of which is dated 20 Feb.,
JUNE. and the imprint June 1553.

1558. Nov. 17. Elizabeth succeeds to the throne.

1559. SEPT. A second edition of *Regni Papistici* is published at Basle.

NOV. 24. The date of Gasper Heywood's poetical preface to his translation of Seneca's *Thyestes*, the printing of which was finished on 25 March 1560. In this preface, he supposes himself to meet Seneca, while in a dream, whom he thus addresses. [The allusions are important as showing the rage for translating then prevailing; and also as virtually announcing Googe's translation, no portion of which had as yet appeared.]

A labour long (quoth I) it is that riper age doothe craue
And who shall trauaile in thy bookes, more iudgement ought to haue
Then I: whose greener yeares therby no thanks may hope to wynne.
Thou seest dame Nature yet hath sette no heares vppon my chynne
Craue this therefore of grauer age, and men of greater skill
Full many be that better can, and some perhapps that will.
But yf thy will be rather bent a yong mans witt to proue,
And thinkst that elder lerned men perhaps it shall behoue,
In woorks of weight to spende theyr tyme, goe where Mineruaes men,
And finest witts doe swarme: whome she hath taught to passe with pen,
In Lyncolnes Inne and Temples twayne, Grayes Inne and other mo,
Thou shalt them fynde whose paynfull pen thy verse shall flourishe so,
That Melpomen thou wouldst well weene had taught them for to wright,
And all their works with stately style, and goodly grace t'endite,
There shalt thou see the selfe same Northe, whose woorke his witte displayes,
And Dyall dothe of Princes paynte, and preache abroad his prayse.
There Sackuyldes Sonetts sweetely sauste, and featly fyned bee,
There Norton's ditties do delight, there Yeluertons doo flee
Well pewrde with pen: suche yong men three, as weene thou mightest agayne,
To be begotte as Pallas was, of mightie Ioue his brayne.
Then heare thou shalt a great reporte of Baldwyns worthie name
Whose Myrrour doth of Magistrates, proclayme eternall fame.
And there the gentle Blunduille is by name and eke by kynde,

Of whome we learne by Plutarches lore, what frute by Foes to fynde.
There Bauande bydes, that turnde his toyle a Common welthe to frame,
And greater grace in Englyshe geues, to woorthy authors name,
There Googe a gratefull gaynes hath gotte, reporte that runneth ryse
Who crooked Compasse dothe describe, and Zodiake of lyfe.
And yet great nombre more, whose names yf I shoulde now resight,
A ten tymes greater woorke then thine, I should be forste to wright.

BARNABY GOOGE, son of Robert Googe, esq. recorder of Lincoln, by Margaret his wife, daughter of Sir John Mantell, was born in or about 1540, at Alvingham, Lincolnshire. He was some time a member of Christ's College in this university, but does not appear to have graduated here. He was also of New College, Oxford. Upon leaving college, he travelled through France to Spain. . . . . By his wife he had issue Matthew; Thomas; Robert, Fellow of All Souls' College, Oxford; Barnaby, master of Magdalen College, Cambridge; Francis; William; Anne; Mary. *Cooper. Athen. Cantab.* ii. 39. *Ed.* 1858.

1559 The first of the translations of Seneca; *Troas*, by T. Heywood, published.

1560. APR. or MAY. There is the following entry in the Stationer's Registers "Recevyd of Raufe newbery, for his lycense for printing of a boke called pallengenius, and he geveth to the howse . . iiij^d" J. P. Collier. *Extracts. &c.* i. 26. *Ed.* 1848.

This was *The First thre Bokes of the most Christian poet Marcellus Palingenius called* THE ZODIAKE OF LIFE *Newly translated out of Latin into Englysh.* This edition, which we have been unable to see, Mr. Collier states, in *Bibliographical Catalogue*, "This is one of the rarest poetical works in our language: we never had an opportunity of seeing more than the exemplar before us, and our belief is that only one other copy is in existence.' *ii.* 88. *Ed.* 1865. Mr. Collier also states that it is dedicated to his grandmother lady Hales, and also to William Cromer, Thomas Honywood and Ralph Heimund Esquires. Herbert states that he styles this piece, 'the first frutes of his study.' *p.* 767. It likewise contains the following initial poems [which we here print from the next edition of 1561]:

The Preface.

When as syr Phebe with backward course, the horned gote had caught,
And had the place from whence he turnes his lofty face out sought:
Amid the entraunce of the grades of Capricorne he stode,
And distant far from him away was Marce with fiery mode,
He lackd th[e]aspect of mighty Ioue and Venus pleasaunt loke
with beames he could not broile from hie for heat his Globe forsoke.
Old Saturne then aloft did lie, with lusty riueled face:
And with a backward course he ranne from out the twinnes apace,
And towardes the Bull he gan to driue intending there to rest,
His croked crabbed cankerd limmes in louely Venus nest.
With frosen face about he loked and vile deformed hewe,
And downe the boysterous Boreas sent in euery coste that blewe,
Who spoylde the pleasant trees of leafe, byreft the ground of grene,
That life in springing springs or plants might no where now be sene:
The liuely sappe forsoke the bowgh and depe the rote it held
And spoyling frutes the flakey snowes on tender bowes they dweld
When down amongest my bokes I sate and close I crouched for cold,
Fayre Ladyes nyne with stately steps alofe I might behold,
In mantels gyrt of comely grace, and bokes in hand they bare,
With Laurell leafe theyr heades were crownd, a sight to me but rare.
I saw them come and vp I rose, as dewty moued to meete
These learned Nimphes, and down I fall before theyr comely feete.
With rosey lippes and shining face and Melpomen her name,
This lady fyrst began to speake, and thus her wordes to frame.
Stand vp yong man, quoth she, dispatch, and take thy pen in hand,
Wryte thou the ciuil warres and broyle in auncient Latines land.

Reduce to English sence she said, the lofty Lucanes verse
The cruel chaunce and dolfull end of Cesars state rehearse.
Maddam (quoth Vrany) with that, in this you do me wrong
To moue my man to serue your turne that hath profesd of long,
And vowed his yeares with me to serue in secreat motions hie,
To beat his brain in searching forth the rowlinges of the sky.
Nay rather take in hand quod she, (and on me ful she lokes)
With English rime to bring to light Aratus worthy bokes.
Describe the whirling spheares aboue and mouinges euery one,
How forced about from East to West from West to East they gone:
Aratus verse wil shew the plain how Circles al they run
How glides ye course thorow croked line of Phebe the shining sun.
Wheras the fixed Poles do stay, and where the snake doth crepe,
In heauens hie among the North where beares theyr course do kepe
By this quoth she) thou shalt receiue immortal fame at last,
Much more then if thou shouldst declare those bloudy bankets past.
These wordes declard wyth pleasaunt voyce, this Lady held her peace,
And forth before them all I saw the loueliest Lady prease:
Of stature tal, and Venus face, she semde me thought to haue
And Calliope she called was with verse that wrytes so graue,
Sisters quod she and Ladies all of Ioue his mighty line,
To whom no art doth lie vnknowne that heare we may define:
Chefe patrons of the Poets pore, and aiders of their verse,
Without whose help their simple heds would nothyng well rehearse,
I am become a suter here to you my Ladies all,
For him that heare before you standes as vnto learning thrall,
A Poet late I had whose pen, did tread the crabbed wayes,
Of vertuous life, declaring how that men shoulde spend theyr daies.
In Romish lande he liued longe, and Palingen his name
It was. Whereby he got himselfe an euerlasting fame
Of them that learned be. But of the meane and ruder sorte
He liues vnknowne and lackes therby his iuste and right reporte.
Wherfore my sute is to you all graunte me this wyght a while,
That standeth heare that he may turne my Poetes stately style,
To Vulgar speche in natiue tounge: that all may vnderstande.
To this they all agreed and sayed, take thou that worcke in hande.
Amased then I answered thus good ladies al (quoth I)
Whose Clientes fame, for euer flies and name can neuer dye
Returne your sentence late pronounced call back your wordes agayne,
And let not me take that in hande that I can not attayne.
In Englande here a hundred heddes more able nowe therebe,
Thys same to doe: then chose the beste and let the worste go free.
Best you doe so then that my verse receaue immortall shame,
When I shall paye the price of paynes with hasarde of my name.
With this they all began to frowne and wholy with on[e] voice.
Take thou this same in hande thei crie, thou hast none other choyse.
And fast away from me thei fling, as halfe in angry moode
Thei lefte me thus in wofull case: whereas a while I stoode,
And mused what I best might do, at last my pen I tooke
Commaunded thus to English heare, this famous Poets booke.
Now since that I haue thus begunne, you (learned) I requyre:
With your dispraise or great dysdaine quenche not this kyndled fyre:
But geue me rather cause to ende, this worke so late begonne,
So shall I thinke and well bestowde my paynes when all is done.

¶ The booke to the reader.

WHo sekes to shun ye shattring sails of mighty Momus mast,
Must not attempt ye sugred seas, where muses ancour cast.
For Momus there doth ryde at flote, with scornefull tonges yfraght:
With cancred cracks of wrathfull words he keeps the passage straught.
That none without disdaine may passe where muses nauie lies,
But straight on them with ireful mode the scornful God he flies

Since none may scape, I am not he, that can my self assure:
Through surging seas of depe disdaine my passage to procure.
But am content for to receiue reproche at Momus hand:
Syth none there is, that may the nose of Rhynocere withstand.
The learned wyttes I heare requyre with rigour not to iudge
The common sort I noughte esteme vnskilful though they grudge.
Nor few of them can hold theyr peace but finde them selues a doe,
In vewing workes as he that sought, to mende Appelles shoe.
Both sortes I wish if that they would contented to remaine,
And beare the weaknes of my wit and not therat disdaine.

1561. In this year there appeared the second edition of Googe's translation of the *Zodiacus Vitæ*, containing the first six books, see *p.* 90. and also the following poem, which Mr. Collier states is not in the first edition.

IF Chaucer nowe shoulde liue, whose eloquence deuine,
Hath paste ye poets al that came of auncient Brutus lyne,
If Homere here might dwell, whose praise the Grekes resounde
If Vergile might his yeares renewe, if Ouide myght be founde:
All these myght well be sure theyr matches here to fynde.
So much dothe England florishe now with men of Muses kynde.
Synce these might find their mates, what shame shall this my ryme
Receaue, that thus I publishe here in such a perlous tyme?
A Poet ones there lyued, and Cherill *was hys name:*
Who thought of Alexanders actes to make immortal fame.
Bredde vp in Pegase *house, of Poetes auncient bloude:*
A thousande verses yll he made, and none but seuen good.
Sythe Homer, Virgile, and the rest maye here theyr matches see:
Lett Cherill *not thereat disdayne, he shall be matched with me.*
For eche good verse he dyd receyue a peece of golde (I trowe)
For eche yll verse the kynge did bydde his eare shoulde fele a blowe.
Though I presume with him as mate coequall to remaine:
Yet seake I not herein to be copartener of his gayne.

FINIS.

The above three poems are omitted in all subsequent editions.

The Epitaph on Phaer was probably written before Googe went abroad.

* WINTER. It is apparent from the allusions on *p.* 29, that Googe went towards Spain about this time, leaving these *Eglogs, &c.* in the hands of his friend Blundeston.

1562. PENTECOST [MAY 17 &c.] Blundeston writes his poetical preface.—See *pp.* 28-30.

MAY 27. He writes his prose preface at *pp.* 26, 27, and leaves all with the printer.

1562-3? WINTER. Googe reaches home from Spain, while Blundeston is away from London. *p.* 25; on whose return, he is astonished to learn that his poems are in the printers' hands, and the paper provided for the impression. Yielding at length to his friend's persuasion he suffers them to appear: finishing *Cupido's conquered* as he states at *p.*

1563. MAR. 15. 25 The printing is therefore finished on 15 March 1563, as stated on the Title at *p.* 19, and Colophon at *p.* 128.

APR. 28. A. Neville's translation of Seneca's *Œdipus*, is finished by T. Colwell, who also printed these *Eglogs, &c.*

We now come to the story of Googe's love, troublous courtship and marriage. There are traces at *pp.* 87, 99 of an earlier and unrequited attachment to Mistress A., previous to his voyage to Spain, but it is his winning of Mary Darrell with which we have now to do. Some preliminary facts must be first touched upon.

What had occurred prior we are unable to say. Only one short poem to Maystresse D[arrell] occurs in this collection (*i.e.* before March 1563): and that is marked by the most delicate respectfulness: but the strange struggle of the two Kentish families with Cecil and Archbishop Parker came about in this way. John Lennard, Esq. [*b.* 1509—*d.* 12. Mar. 1590. æt. 81] of Chevening, (N.E. of Tunbridge Wells), was a rich prosperous man of 54 years of age, Prothonotary of the Common Pleas, and possessed of many lands and manors in four other counties besides Kent. [Hasted's *Kent.* 359-360. *Ed.* 1778.] His eldest of two sons, Sampson Lennard [*b.* 1545—*d.* 20 Sept. 1615] aged 18, was head over ears in love with Mary Darrell. Now the Darrell family, originally from Yorkshire, lived at Scotney, a manor house in Lamberhurst parish, which is the southernmost parish of that county and adjoins Sussex. They were of lesser note and wealth than the Lennards. Thomas Darrell had married twice. By his first wife, he had a daughter: by his second, Mary Roydon, daughter of —— Roydon Esq[re] of East Peckham, he had one son, Henry: and four daughters, Mary, Googe's sweetheart; Eleanor; Frances; and Margaret. [Hasted's *Kent.* ii. 380. *Ed.* 1782]

Googe had been a long time a visitor at Scotney, certainly before the publication of this work, as the poem above referred to witnesses: but he does not seem to have betrothed himself till the summer of this year. The curious correspondence on this subject opens first with the two following letters from Sir William Cecil, the drafts of which corrected by him, are in the State Paper Office.

1563. OCT. 1. *Mem. of my Master's letters to Mr Lennard for Bar. Googe.* Mr Lennard I haue ben certifyed by Googe who being my servant is also my kinsman that whereas there hath of late passed an agreement between him and the daughter of Mr Thomas Darrell in Kent as concerning marriage having her friends consent herein as I understand by her fathers letters written vnto him which I have read and being thoroughly at a poynt for all things between them He hath of late by your means been hindered to his great grief as also against all due order of well using whereby he hath declared vnto me that minding to do vnto him so great an iniury your opinion is that he is vtterly destitute of friends and that I make no other account of him but as of one of my men. Whereas I esteeme him as my near kinsman and so he shalbe sure to find me in any reasonable case Wherefore I pray you herrin to vse him no otherwise than one whom I well esteem. I haue seen the letters that haue passed between her father and him as also her own letters whereby the matter is made clear vnto me that she hath fully assured herself vnto him."

Knowing what we do of Sir William Cecil's soundness of judgment: the circumstances must have been very strong in favour of Googe before he could have thus written: and as also in the following letter to Mr Darrell.

"After my very hearty commendations. Where as I understand that Googe my servant hath been a sutor to your daughter moved chiefly as I take it by the virtuous report of her and the friendly entertainment that he found at your hands, as both by his information and certain your letters written to him I understand since he hath so far provided that there hath assurance passed between them evidently to be proved by his allegation and her own letters. These shall be to require you not to go about to break the bond so perfectly knit between them, whereof you have been so long a favorer. Considering that you knew as well his estate for living at the first as at any time since and allthough his living be not great ye shall not need to fear that he lacketh friends and wellwishers. Being both my kinsman and my servant. Thus I require you to show him such friendship as you have done before as you would require any frendship at my hands. I haue thought to haue written to my Lord of Canterbury to have made an end of the matter but I trust my letters to you in this case shall be sufficient."

Mr Lennard's own reply to the Secretary of State's request, is now *Lansdowne MS.* 7 *p.* 70-83.

1563. NOV. 10. My duety done vnto your honor. Your lettre directed to me touching master Googe was delyvered a moneth after the date thereof to a boye of my howse by a ploughe boy. The cause not yours but master Googes. I hasted the lesse to sende the answer for lacke of his messenger: The matter not worth my sending saving to satisfie you The effect of your lettre is that master Googe hath enformed you that he is hindred by my meanes concerning his mariage with master Darrell his daughter and that my opinion is that he is destitute of frendes and that you accompte not of him but as of one of your men. Ye write further that the matter is made plaine to you by the maides lettres and her fathers which you haue sene and redde that she hath assured her selfe to master Googe: and in asmuche as it hath pleased you so to put the one side, it occasioneth me to offer to you th[e]other to that ende which els I woulde not for the tedyousnes thereof, which may not be shortened.

I praie you doubte not that I haue good will to pleasure any man of yours muche more your honest kyndesman. There is cause why I shoulde, you being my good Master. But for this marrage I myght and must haue done with honesty as I did, with reuerence I speake it, though it had touched your sonne or the best subiecte in this Realme.

I knowe not master Googe who as he hath sclaundered me to you for your accompting of him being hidden to me, so vntruely and scornefully he as one that seemeth to haue a whotte hedde and a sicke braine wrote to me this somer past that by the extreme highte of my promysed mountaines master Darrell had altered his mynde from him and for riches sake ment to matche his daughter with my sonne and that frendes of the best which shoulde be able to beare strooke with the best of his aduersaries shoulde do and write in the cause. He hath also mysused me in an other lettre the copy is here inclosed. They that knowe him and my sonne thyncke aswell or better of my sonne as of him to all respectes. And there were not cause why I would wyshe my son buryed. Mountaynes be lyke I promysed none, for master Darrell will confesse that he and his wyfe before master Googes sute, were earnest suters to me and that their daughter was as forwarde in desire as woman hedde would gene leue to matche my sonne: and that I never commended but still disabled my sonne to them all thre and they all thre as fast habiled and commended my sonne.

Master Darrell telleth me that vppon your lettre sent to him for master Googe he wrote to you that his promyse his wifes and daughters were past them to me for my sonne before master Googes sute and that the talke which he had with master Googe thereof happened by his mystaking of a lettre of myne. He wrote truely to you therein which clereth me.

I had divers talkes with the maide for my sonne in his absence and yet no mo then she was glad of and then delyvered me by her parents. And hereto I call god to witnesse that not withstandyng my obieccions (as of purpose to trye her I moued many to longe to be recyted here) that myght haue stayed her from matching with my sonne; so farre was she from a nay that she neuer offred any delay to be my sonnes wif but was most desirous of it in worde and gesture: so that at our last talke, hearynge her mylde and loving answers will full consent to haue my sonne who I know loved her entierly and therefore I hauing good lyking in me that he shoulde be her husband, nature wrought in me for her to lay my ryght hande on her brest and to speake thus in effecte *then I see that with gods helpe the frute that shall come of this body shall possesse all that I haue, and therevpon I will kyss you.* And so in dede I kyssed her. I gaue her after this, silke for a gowne (she neuer wore none so good), and she in token of her good will gave my sonne a handkercher and in affirmance of this her father wrote a letter to me by her consent he saith and that he redde the lettre to her, the copy is here inclosed that declareth her full consent to be my sonnes wife.

Master Darrell dwelleth from me nere xx myles a way that I never vsed but for this purpose and then in somer and at my comyng thither at Bartholomewetide last I tolde the parents and maide that I hearde say she shoulde haue a husband whereat I merveiled considering the talke that had past betweene vs. They all thre answered me and others for me very often that it was not so and that master Googe was but a suter To prove that to be true the parents sent me afterward a copy herinclosed of the maides lettre sent to master Googe of late wherein she termeth him to be but a suter and prayeth him to leue his sute and the parents still say that he hath no holde of her except that by secrete intysement ageinst their wills he hath caught some worde of her, a thynge odyous to god and not to be favoured by man.

Now if the talke that she had with me had beene to my sonne it had ben a full contracte but my sonne being absent it is not soo. Yet is it suche matter as therevpon he myght the rather be a suter as master Googe is for it is no rare thynge for one woman to haue dyuers suters at ones.

Thus haue I made you a true discourse of all my doings, which I trust you in whose iudgement I durst put all my lande, lyving, and lyfe can not iudge to be ageine any due order of well vsing thoughe by master Googes false informaccion ye write in your lettre to me to be ageinst all due order of well vsing.

I shoulde be no geyner by this my sonnes matching but should haue forgone a M marks with matching in as good a stocke in the countrey where I dwell, and sithens suche encumbrance is wrought as I perceyue there ys on the maides part who as I here wavereth in this case I and my sonne may with honestie geue vp our sute therein for I were to madde to matche my eldest sonne where any entangling is and no stedfastnes at all I pray you thyncke not that I woulde so do as surely I wold not for any treasure in this worlde And so I knytte vpp that thoughe she woulde my sonne surely he will not haue her and I say that he shall not haue her.

Master Googe by fyrst talke with me vppon good cause showed might haue staied my sonnes sute soner then by sawsy lettres some sent by ruffians Yf I sought to marry a beggers daughter I wolde therein offer her father no despite. Master Darrell sayeth that master Googe vseth him so evell seking aide at his ennemyes hande in the countrey about him and hath faced him that he wolde tell the Quene of him and that a seriaunt at armes shoulde fetche his daughter from him and that you shoulde fetche her within a month with a number of other straunge dealings which haue troubled the gentleman muche.

And so I leave to trouble you Wishinge you increase of honor At Chevening the xth of November 1563.

Your seruaunt assuredly to command I. lennard.

ENDORSED.—*To the right honourable and his very good Master Sir William Cecil knyght chefe Secretary to the Quenes maiestie.*

Lansdowne MSS. 7. *p.* 79-83.

The three enclosures of Mr. Lennard's letter are as follows:—

ENCLOSURE A. *The effect of one of moster darells letters sent to master Lennard, which as master Darrell yet sayethe he wrate by his daughters consent. And dyd read yt to her and so sent yt to master lennard.*

After my ryght harty commendations etc. presumynge of youre good wyll and goodnes towardes my daughter mary: althoughe that before yat I moued ye mariage, betwene youre sonne and her I knewe ryght well yat it was my daughters goodwyll and desire to haue it to come to passe: and so moued it by her consent and desire. Yet accordinge to youre godly admonition in youre letter, I haue agayne fully trauayled with her therein: and fynde her moste wyllyng and desirouse to matche with youre sonne, so yat she is truly master Sampsonnes: who shalbe sure to haue of her a louynge and obedient wife, and you and mastres Lennarde an obedient daughter. And although nature myghte moue my tonge and penne, to say and write muche in fauour of my daughter, yet as god shall iudge me in this case, if I knewe any spotte in her I would expresse it to you: she is truly gods seruaunt, and I trust yat he wyll so preserue her. &c. &c.

Your louynge friend T. Darrell.

ENDORSED.—*A copy of ye effect of one of master Darrelles letters, sent to master Lennard.*

ENCLOSURE B—*A copy of Marye Darelles letter sent to master Goge.*

After my harty commendations gentle master Googe where you haue binne and yet do continue a Sutor to me in ye waye of maryage whereunto nether presentlye I haue nor I am well assured shall haue, ye good wyll or consent of father nor mother to whome I am both by ye lawe of god and nature bound to geue honoure and obedyence, and in no wyse wyllyngly to greue or offend them. And do well consider yat my chefe obedience and dutye towardes them, is to be bestowed in maryage by there consentes, and to there good contentation Assurynge my selfe in meditation and thinkynge hereof. hereof yat beynge there obedient chylde and to them most bounden in disobayenge them therein, I shall not only be depriued from yat blessinge, which god hath promised to suche as truly honor there parentes, but allso shalbe assured to fynde and haue ye like disobedience of my chyldren: yf euer god shall geue me any: which by godes grace I wyll eschue. Wherefore I hartely beseche you ientle master Googe, if euer any true loue or goodwyll you haue borne towarde me, cease and leave of from all further sute or meanes to me in this matter, lettynge you to wete yat knowynge my parentes myndes to ye contrarye hereof, I wyll in no wyse match with you in any case. And thus wisshinge to you, in other place to matche accordynge to your own hartes desire, and to youre farre greter aduauncemente, I bid you farewell. From my fathers house at Scotney this thursday the. xxth of octobre. Marye Darell.

ENDORSED.—*A copy of marye Darrells but sent to master Goge, verye latelye.*

ENCLOSURE C.

Ryght worshipfull and my louynge frindes I haue receaued youre letters wherein you write yat you perfectly understand ye hole state of ye case yat hath passed betwene master lennard and youre cosinne mary before my acquayntaunce with her, even so have I binne certyfied of a pretye laffynge toye as touchynge a precontracte declarynge at full ye sharp inuencyon of master lennardes graue hedd, whereat if old Democritus were now alyue, I would thynke yat he should haue iuster cause ta laffe then at his contrymens folly. Ye seame to wyll a meatynge to be had betwene vs, whereunto I with all my hart consent, althoughe a number consyderyng my case would not doe, consyderynge the martiall furniture yat hath benne prepared ageynst me, and ye Italyon inuentyons yat haue binne menaced towardes me, which when ye counsell shal vnderstande, I trust they will not altogether commend. For all this, takyng you to be my verye fryndes, I reioyse to meate you, neither if my aduersaryes should be in commission, would I feare to see them. Of one thyng I must craue pardonne, for not beynge able to meate you on sundaye because I haue sent my manne to ye courte, who wyll retorne on munday as I trust, but whether he do or not, I wyll with godes leaue wayte vppon you at yat daye in hast from Dongeon [or Done gone, a manor house close to Canterbury, at this time the residence of his grandmother Margaret, now a widow of her *third* husband, Sir James Hales, who died in 1558], the xvith of octobre. Youre louynge frynd Barnabe Goge.

ENDORSED.—*A copy of a scornefull letter written by master Goge, to master George Darrell and master Edward Darrell.*

From all this it is clear that the Darrell parents were basely striving their very utmost to make their daughter Mary give up her true love and to match for money. Here was the girl in grief and dismay withstanding the alternate solicitations and threats of her own parents and the attempted hold on her of John Lennard. The matter did not, however, stop with his correspondence. It went before Archbishop Parker, who refers to it in the following letter to Cecil, dated 'thys Saturdaye at night beyng the xxth of Nouembre.'

1563. NOV. 19. "Yt may please your honor to vnderstand that I haue grete cause most humblye to gyue the Queens Maiesty thankes, for the fauor showed toward my request for the preferment of my chaplen and so like wise I hartely thanke your instancye therein as by your letters I vnderstand. Wherein ye wryght for your cosyn and seruaunt Barnaby Goge to haue his matter heard according to Lawe and equytie) which matter as yesterdaye I haue examined a[d]visedly, having not only the yong Gentlewoman before me to vnderstond of her self the state of the cause, who remayneth fyrme and stable to stond to that contract which she hath made, as also her father and mother: whom I find, the most ernest parents against the bargain as I could see.

In fyne I haue sequestered her out of both their handes into the custodye of one Mr. *Tuften* a right honest gentleman. vntyl, the precontract, which is by hir parents alleged for one Leonards son, a protonotary be induced But this maye giue occasion to bryng it in to the Arches to spend moneye how be yt I meane to dull that expectation and to go *plane et summarie* to worke, to spare expences, which Mr Leonard and the wilful parents wuld fayne incur to wery the yong Gentleman, paraventure not superfluously monyed so to sayle the seas with them." *Lands. MS.* 6. *p.* 130.

It is thoroughly satisfactory to find that the parental combination broke down, and that at last, though in 1564 or 1565, two such constant lovers became man and wife.

1565. JAN. Googe's final and complete translation of Manzolli's poem appeared. From the *Epistle Dedicatorie* to Sir W. Cecil, we extract the following:—

"The fauorable accepting of my simple trauayles lately dedicated vnto your honor, hath so much boldened and thorowelye encouraged me, that mawgre the despite of most reprochfull tongs, I haue not feared to finish the course of my long pretended race: with no lesse profite as I trust, vnto a number, than paynefull trauayle vnto my selfe. Wherein if I had knowen at the firste, as much as since I haue perfectly vnderstode, neyther had I as then taken vpon me so great an enterprise, nor since so rudely finished, the translation of so eloquent a Poet. For when I fyrste began to employ some part of my leysure aboute it, making dilligente inquirie, I could learne of no man that euer had attempted to english the same. So that perceyuing my labour to be no hindraunce to any other mans prayse, and lamenting to see so Christian a writer to lie hyd and vnknowen to the ignoraunt sorte, I thought I should not do amisse, if al that in me lay I bestowed, in the albeit simple and slender, yet faythfull and true translation, of so vertuous a worke. But since I haue certaynely vnderstoode, that when I firste began to fall in hand wythall, three bookes thereof were both eloquentely and excellently englished, by Master Smith, clark vnto the most honorable of the Queenes Maiesties counsell. Whose doings, as in other matters I haue wyth admiration beholde, so in thys I am well assured I should with an amased minde haue seene: I would that eyther I had latelier begonne it, or else that he had fallen in hand sooner with it, whereby my grosse and homely style might haue bene no hindrance to the fruites of so pure a penne. But since it was my fortune, so blindely to venture vpon it, I truste my trauayle shall neuer the more be enuied. I could not (when I had long debated ye matter with myselfe) finde out a Poet more meete for the teaching of a Christian life (an estate in these oure dayes most miserably decayed than this no lesse learned than famous Italion: *Marcellus Pallingenius*, a man of such excellent learning and Godly life, that neither ye vnquietnesse of his time (Italie in those dayes raging wyth most cruell and bloudy warres), ne yet the furious tyranny of the Antichristian Prelate (vnder whose ambicious and Tirannicall gouernaunce he continually liued) coulde once amase the *Muse*, or hinder the zealous and vertuous spirit of so Christian a Souldiour. I haue many times much mused wyth my self, howe (liuing in so daungerous a place) he durst take vpon him so boldely to controll the corrupte and vnchristian liues of the whole Colledge of contemptuous Cardinals, the vngracious ouerseeings of bloudthyrsty Bishops, the Panchplying practises of pelting Priours, the manifold madnesse of mischeuous Monkes, wyth the filthy faternitie of flattering Friers. Which surely he durst neuer haue done, but onely that he was heartened wyth a happy and heauenly spirite. Which notable audacitie of his was wonderfully reuenged by the malicious hands of such as felt themselues fretted with his spiritual corsey. For when they had no power to execute their tyrannie vpon his innocent body in time of his life, their mischieuous malice was no whit ashamed to consume with fyre the blamelesse bones of so vertuous a man: yea and that a great while after his death. Besides the reprouing of the leud liues of the Clergie, he boldly inueyed agaynst the gracelesse gouernance of proud pompous Princes, ye licencious liuing of the riottous nobilitie, the couetous catchings of greedy Lawyers, the vngodly gaynes of foolish Physitians, and the corrupted consciences of deceytful Artificers: affirming playnly, that if they did not better beautify their christian names with a more christian life, of so many thousands as haue in vaine receiued that most holy sacrament of sacred Baptisme, there should scarce three aspire vnto the enheritance of Heauenly ioyes. What doth your honor suppose this man would haue written? Vnto how great a volume doe you thinke his works would haue amounted, if so that GOD had appoynted him to florish at this present time in England, wheras pitifully raigneth such monstrous and horrible pride, such cancred and spiteful malice, such false and fayned friendships, such lack of loue and charity, such professing of God in words, and denying him in works, as doubtlesse is not to to be found among the faythlesse Turks, miscreant Sarazens, or superstitious Iewes? . . .

I would therfore wish that we should not to much presume of the securitie obtayned by a Christian name, but that we should wyth our endeuour apply our selues to shew such fruits as duetie requireth in the followers of Christe. Whereby we shoulde not onely preuayle agaynst our enemies, and stoppe the mouths of our slaunderous aduersaries, but also enjoy a blessed and happy tranquility in this worlde, and be assured to obtayne the promised pleasures in the worlde to come. For the teachinge whereof, I know no man that hath so much trauayled and perfectly profyted, as hath this Poet, which here present vnto your honor.

1570. Googe's translation of Kirchmeyer's poem appears dedi-
1574-1575. cated to Queen Elizabeth, under the title of *The Popish Kingdome or reigne of Antichrist.*

1572. OCT. 18. Dame Hales, Googe's maternal grandmother dies.

There are no less than twenty autograph letters of Googe between these years in the State Paper Office calendered under S. P. Domestic. *Ireland.* Googe--who held the patent of Provost Marshal to the Court of Connaught --was sent over by Lord Burleigh to watch Irish affairs. Most of these letters will be found in the life of Googe contributed by Mr. Pinkerton to *Notes and Queries.* 3rd S. iii.

1576. He published a revised text of his translation of the *Zodiacus vitæ.*

1577. He published a translation from the Latin of the *Four Bokes of Husbandrie* of Conrad Heresbachius. The preface is dated Kingston [upon Hull?] January 1577.

1578. A second edition of this book appeared.

1579. He supplied a prose address to B. Rich's *Allarme to England.*

1579. He published a translation from the Spanish of *The Proverbs* of Inez Lopez de Mendoza, Marquis of Santillana.

1586. A third edition of his revision of Heresbachius appears.

1588. A second edition of his revised text of his translation of Palingenius appeared.

T. Warton, *Hist. of E. P.* states on authority of the Coxeter MSS. that Googe also translated Aristotle's *Categories.*

I am indebted to Mr. C. Bridger, Hon. Member of the Soc. of Ant. of Newcastle, for the following information respecting Googe's death.

1594. FEB. Barnabee Goche of Alvingham, co. Lincoln. Esq. Inq. post. mort. taken at Lowth 6 Oct. 36. Eliz: died circa 7 Feb. 36. Eliz: Matthew Goche his son and heir then 28 years old.

FEB. 16. Barnabas Goche of Alvingham, co. Lincoln. Administration granted to Mary Goche his relict. *Perog. Ct. of Cant.*

INTRODUCTION.

THe continuity of the Art of Poefy in this country has been unbroken from the time of Chaucer to our own day. Not that great or even confiderable Poets have overlapped one another in a continuous fucceffion: but there have never wanted thofe who, according to the gift that was in them, have perpetually reprefented by their Song, beauty of expreffion, refinement of ideas, ethereality of fancy, vigour of fatire, or the paffion and merriment of human life. During no portion of this time has England been wholly deftitute of true Poetry, or barren of real 'makers.'

2. In comparifon with the literary fplendour and glory that crowned the laft days of Elizabeth, the early years of her reign might feem poor and ftunted in mind. But it is only with *fuch* a comparifon; one which alfo dwarfs not only earlier but later ages. Actually, the firft two decades of this reign are a general advance in this branch of literature on the two previous reigns, and more efpecially exhibit a fharp rebound from the oppreffivenefs of the government of Philip and Mary.

Therefore, juft as we delight to fearch out the fountain head, and to trace the early ftreamlets of a mighty river which, in its full ftrength, may carry on its bofom world of wealth for the ufe and pleafure of man; fo it behoves us clofely to fcan thefe firft buddings of a free literature in the genial fpring-tide of the new Queen's reign; now that the furious ftorms of religious and intellectual oppreffion had paffed away: and fo to trace out the works of that race of writers who were the heralds, the forerunners, the teachers of Spenfer,

Shakespeare, and Johnson, and their glorious phalanx of contemporary poets.

We have said 'general' advance, because Tottel's *Miscellany* of 1557 is, in its varied excellence, the substantive beginning of modern English verse. Yet that collection represents the poetical gleanings of three entire reigns, and is exceptional from the general literature of the time in which it was printed. But with the new Queen poesy came into fashion, and almost all the young gentlemen of the Inns of Court tried their prentice hands at it.

3. As in spring-tide we gather flowers rather than fruits, so in this earlier literature we must look for imperfect Assays rather than finished Masterpieces. Most modern literatures have commenced with translations, imitations, and the like. At this time there was quite a rage for translating. The riches of old classical thought and style; the charms of Italian and Spanish fiction; history, morals, tragedies, romances both in prose and verse; with translated poems, constituted the staple of English polite literature at this time. With this there was the constant accretion of *The Mirrour for Magistrates*, and also, though not to any large extent, original lighter verse, as in the present work and also George Turberville's *Epitaphes, Epigrams, Songs, and Sonets*, of which there are believed to have been three editions by 1570; of the earliest of which no copy is at present known.

4. Associating with many of these translators, himself distinguished for his English version of Manzolli's *Zodiacus Vitæ*, Barnabe Googe, a young gentleman of 20 to 23 years of age, fresh from college, wrote for his private delectation most of the contents of this Reprint. How his friend Blundeston sent what he had written to the 'poor printer,' with two prefaces of his own, about

Whitfuntide 1562, and how Googe in 1563 came at length to acquiefce in their completion and publication, is fufficiently told by themfelves in the prefaces, and need not be here repeated.

5. It is noteworthy that there was a general habit about this time of cutting the long twelve or fourteen fyllable line into two, fo that the rhyme only occurs on the fecond and fourth lines. This is noticeable in the early tranflations of Seneca between 1500-1560, by Jafper Heywood, Alexander Neville (a contributor alfo to this volume), John Studley, Thomas Nuce, and Thomas Newton, as alfo in the poetical works of George Turberville and others. The fole reafon for this would feem to have been to print on a fmall page of paper; for in some of thefe works poems do occafionally occur in fmaller type with fuch lines at full length.

6. In the ftory of Englifh literature this most rare volume occupies an important place from its epitaphs of Phaer and Grimaold, both of them tranflators; and its Sonnets to Dean Nowell, Bifhop Bale, and Richard Edwards 'of the Chappel.' Some of thefe have been printed by Mr. Collier in his *Bibliographical Catalogue;* but the work, as a whole, has never been printed fince 15th March 1563. Cordial thanks are due and tendered to Mr. Huth for the loan of his copy for this edition.

7. This fmall Collection is alfo interefting as being to a large extent native verfe, though on the Italian model. It was undoubtedly in much fuperinduced by Tottel's *Mifcellany*, to which it is in nature and quality the next in time; being itfelf fucceeded by Turberville's *Epitaphs, Epigrams, &c.*, and that by a fucceffion of fimilar works, until the appearance of Francis Davifon's *Poetical Rhapfody* of 1602.

8. One very noticeable feature of Googe's compoſitions in this volume is his earneſt Proteſtantiſm. He had known ſome good Shepheards Daphnes or Alexis, that had flamed in the fire of the Maryan perſecution. Almoſt all his publications are ſtrongly anti-Romaniſt. Taught by the Reformers of Edward VI.'s time, horrified at the cruelties of Mary's reign; Googe repreſents both the intellectual and moral hatred of the young educated Engliſhmen of that time of the entire Papal ſyſtem.

BIBLIOGRAPHY.

Issues in the Author's lifetime.

I.—*As a ſeparate publication.*

1. 1563. London. 1 vol. 8vo. 88 leaves.

There appear to have been printed two title-pages to this work.

Of the three copies known, two are thoſe in the collection of Mr. Huth, and in the Capel collection at Trinity College, Cambridge, have the title as on the oppoſite page; while Mr. W. C. Hazlitt deſcribes, in his *Handbook of Pop. Lit., Ed.* 1867, the title of Mr. Heber's copy, now in the collection of Mr. S. Chriſtie-Miller, at Britwell, thus:
Eglogs, Epytaphes, and Sonettes by Barnabe Googe. COL. Imprynted at London in S. Brydes-Churchyarde, by Thomas Colwell, for Raufe Newbery; and are to be ſold at his ſhop in Fleteſtreet, a little above the conduit 1563. 15 die Menſis March.
It is alſo to be noted that the firſt two alſo vary between themſelves at the beginning of *Egloga ſeptima*: ſee p. 56.

Issues since the Author's death.

I. *As a ſeparate publication.*

2. 1871. DEC. 1. *Engliſh Reprints*: ſee title on *p.* 1.

Eglogs

Epytaphes, and *Sonettes.*

Newly written by

Barnabe Googe:

1563.

15. Marche.

¶ Imprynted at London, by
Thomas Colwell, for Raffe
Newbery, dwelyng in
Fleetstrete a litle a=
boue the Conduit
in the late shop
of Thomas
Bartelet.

¶ *Alexander Neuyll.*

THe Mountaines hie the bluſtryng winds
The fluds: ye Rocks withſtand
The Cities ſtrong, the Cannons ſhot,
and threatning Cheiſtains hand.
The Caſtels houge by longe beſeyge,
and dredfull battrye brooke, [thumps
Bothe fyre, and flames, and thundrynge
and euery deadly ſtroke,
With feruent broylyng furious rage,
doth beate, and dryue to groun
The long defenced wals by force,
and throughly them confound.
Ryght ſo thy Muſe (O worthy *Googe.*)
thy pleaſaunt framed ſtyle
Diſcouerd lyes to momiſh Mouthes
Reprochfull tongs and vyle
Diffaming minds. Regard them not.
preas thou for hygher prayſe.
Submit thy ſelfe to perſons graue,
whoſe Iudgement ryght alwayes
By Reaſon rulde doth ryghtly iudge,
whom Fancies none can charme,
Which in the moſt Inconſtant brains,
are chyefly wont to ſwarme.
Whom no deſyre of ſylthy gayne,
whom lucre none can moue
From truth to ſtray. Such men eſteam,
Such ſuch embrace and loue.
On ſuch men ſtay thy tender years,
ſuch Patrons ſeeke to chuſe.
Which taught by Tyme, and practiſde Proofe
vprighteſt iudgement vſe.
But as for thoſe Crabſnowted beſtes
thoſe ragyng feends of Hell.
Whoſe vile, malicious, hatefull mindes,
with boylyng Rancour ſwell.

Which pufe with Pryde, enflamd with ſpight,
  and drownd in deape diſdain:
Lyke *Momus* monſtrous broode outright
  euen of a ielows Brayn
With curious, canckard, carping mouthes,
  moſt famous dedes diffame,
Defacing thoſe whoſe labours great,
  Deſerue immortall name.
Such crabfaced, cankerd, carliſh chuffs
  within whoſe hatefull breſtes,
Suche Malice bydes, ſuche Rancour broyles,
  ſuch endles Enuy reſts
Eſteame thou not. No preiudice
  to thee: nor yet opreſt,
Thy famous wrytynges are by them.
  Thou lyueſt and euer ſhalt.
Not all the ſlaundryng tonges aliue,
  may purchaſe blame or fault
Vnto to thy name (O worthy *Googe.*)
  No tyme, no fyrye flame
Not all the furies frettyng Force,
  Thy doynges may dyffame.
Let them in broyle of burning ſpight,
  continuall Toyle ſuſtayne
Let them fele ſcourging Plags of mind
  Let euer duryng payne,
Spred through their poiſoned vaines.
  with payſe of dedly waight: Let Care
Oppreſſe theyr vyle infected Harts,
  with ſtynging Malyce fraight.
Let them deſtroy them ſelvs in Time.
  In Rancour let them boyle.
Let mortall hate, let pynching gryeſe,
  let flamyng torments broyle,
Within theyr greuous vexed breſts,
  for euermore to dwell
Let them fele Enuies curſed force,
  (conſumyng Feend of Hell.)

Defye them all. μισάνθρωποι
  and ſquynteyd Monſters ryght
They are. In ſyne leue Sow to ſwill
  and Chuff to canckerd Spyght.
But thou procede in vertuous dedes,
  and as thou haſte begon,
Go forward ſtyll to aduaunce thy fame
  Lyfes Race halfe ryghtly ron
Farre eaſyer tis for to obtain,
  the Type of true Renowne.
Like Labours haue been recompenſt
  with an immortall Crowne.
By this doth famous *Chaucer* lyue,
  by this a thouſande moore
Of later yeares. By this alone
  the olde renowmed Stoore
Of Auncient Poets lyue. By this
  theyr Praiſe, aloſt doth mownt.
Vnto the Skyes: and equall is
  with Stars aboue. Accownt
Thy ſelfe then worthy of the lyke,
  yf that thou doſte proceade
By famous deds thy Fame to enhaunce
  and name abroade to ſpreade.
With Courage ſtout than through the thikſt
  thou needſt not for to feare.
Nor he that ſayth, but he that doth,
  ought *Gloryes* Garlande weare.
Thus ſhalt you ſtyll augment thy name,
  and wyn the hyghe Renowne,
And preſent Prayſe, in preſent Lyfe,
  and after Death a Crowne
Of Honour, that for euer laſts.
  immortall *Fame* in fyne.
To whoſe reward, thy faithfull Frend
  doth wholly the reſygne.

❡ *Finis.*

[On the next page in the original Edition, are the arms of Barnabe Googe.]

To the ryght worſhip-full M. William Louelace *Eſquier, Reader of Grayes Inne:* (Barnabe Googe) *wyſſheth health.*

HOwe lothe I haue ben, beyng of long tyme earneſtlye requyred, to ſuffer theſe tryfles of mine to come to light: It is not vnknowen to a greate nombre of my famyliar acquaintaunce. Who both dayly and hourely moued me therunto, and lytell of long tyme preuayled therin. For I both conſydered and wayed with my ſelfe, the groſenes of my Style: whiche thus commytted to the gaſynge ſhewe of euery eye ſhuld forth with diſcloſe ye manifeſt foly of the Writer, and alſo I feared and miſtruſted the diſdaynfull myndes of a nombre both ſcornefull and carpynge Correctours, whoſe Heades are euer buſyed in tauntyng Iudgementes. Leaſt they ſhuld otherwyſe interprete my doyngs than in deade I meant them. Theſe two ſo great miſchiefes vtterly diſwaded me from the folowynge of my frendes perſwaſions, and wylled me rather to condem them to continuall darkenes, wherby no Inconuenience could happen: than to endaunger my ſelfe in gyuynge them to lyght, to the diſdaynfull doome of any offended mynde. Notwithſtandynge all the dylygence that I could vſe in the Suppreſſion therof coulde not ſuffiſe for I my ſelfe beyng at that tyme oute of the Realme, lytell fearynge any ſuche thynge to happen. A very Frende of myne, bearynge as it ſemed better wyll to my doynges than reſpectyng the hazarde of my name, commytted them all togyther vnpolyſhed to the handes of the Prynter. In whose handes durynge his absence from the Cytie, tyll his returne of late they remayned. At whiche tyme, he declared the matter wholly vnto me: shewynge me, that beynge so farre past, and Paper prouyded for the Impression therof: It coulde not withoute great hynderaunce of the poore Printer be nowe reuoked. His sodayne tale made me at ye fyrst, vtterly amazed, and doubting a great while, what was best to be done: at the lengthe agreyng both with Necessytie and his Counsell, I sayde with *Martiall. iam sed poteras tutior esse domi.* And calling to mynde to whom I myght chieflye commyt the fruytes of my smiling muse: sodaynly was cast before my eyes the perfect vewe of your frendly mynd (gentle Maister Louelace) Vnto whom for the nombred heapes of sundrye Frendshyps, accountynge my selfe as bounde, I haue thought best to gyue them, (not doubtyng) but that they shalbe as well taken, as I do presently meane them.

Desyrynge you herein, as all suche as shall reade them especiallye to beare with the vnpleasaunt forme of my to hastely fynyshed Dreame, the greater part wherof with lytle aduyse I lately ended, because the beginnyng of it, as a senseles head separated from the body was gyuen with the rest to be prynted. And thus desyrynge but for recompence the frendly receyuyng of my slender Gyfte, I ende: wyshynge vnto you good Mayster Louelace in this life the happye enioyeng of prosperous yeares: and hereafter the blessed estate of neuer ceasynge Ioye.

¶ yours assuredly
Barnabe Googe.

[Hereafter follows on the next page the original Edition, a rough woodcut of *Daphnes* and *Amintas*.]

¶ L. Blundeſton *to the Reader.*

TO creepe into thy fauoure (good Reader) with a longe paynted Preamble in prayſe of this Auctor, I account it as vain. The Sonne Beames gyues light ſufficient. To moue thy Affection with forepromyſed pleaſure in reading the volume, I think it as Booteles. Gold is of ſelf force and vertue to draw the deſire. But with flowers of Rethorique ſyrſt to delyght the, or with Pythy Reaſons to wynne thy good wyll and frendlye Reporte for this my attempte: yf ſuche tropes and ſignes were flowing in me to perſwade wel thy fauour or ſo muche Diſcreſcioñ wantynge in the to necglecte my good meanyng, I would eyther enforce my ſelf to vſe a better kynde of perſwaſion or els withdrawe my good wyll from the Sentence of ſo carpynge and ſlender a Iudgement: but as I haue felte no fluddes of the one, ſo likewyſe I ſee no Ebbes of the other, that if I weare no more barraygne of the fyrſte, then fearefull of the laſte: I woulde be then no more ſparynge to horde vp my Treaſure from the: then I truſt to fynd the vnthankfull now in takyng this Preſent from me, which not onely to ſhewe my good wyll, (as my Preface diſcourſeth more largely) by preſeruynge the worthy Fame, and Memorye of my deare frende M. Googe in his abſence I haue preſumed more bouldely to hazard ye pryntyng heareof, though this maye ſuffyce to excuſe well my enterpryſe, but alſo to ſtyrre vp thy Pleaſure and further thy proffit by readyng thefe his workes, whiche here I haue Puplyſhed [? Publyſhed]: openly vnto thee. And ſo (beyng vnſtored my ſelffe) I ſeake to ſateſſie thy learned or willyng deſyre with other mens trauaeiles. But wheare the power fayleth the will may ſuffice, the gyuer, not the gyſt is to be regarded: preferre Colonus Radyſhe roote before the Courtiers barbed horſe.

Accept my goodwyll and way not the valew, ſo ſhalt thou bynd me if power (as it is vnlikely, maye aunſwere hearafter my meanynge, to gratefie thee with the whole fruits of myne owne indeuour and ſo ſhalt thou encourage others to make the partaker of the like or farre greater Iewels who yet doubtyng thy vnthankefull receyte nigardly keape them to their own vſe and priuat commoditie, whear as beynge aſſured of the contrarye by thy frendly report of other mens trauayles, they coulde parhappes be eaſely entreated more frely to lend them abroad to thy greater auayle and furtheraunce. Thus therfore to thy good or euill taking I put foorth this paterne for others to follow in weightyer matters or els to beware by other mens harms, in keaping their names vnreproued by ſylence.

¶ From my Chambre,
the. xxvii. of Maye.
1562.

ℭ *The Preface of* L. Blundeſton.

THE Sences dull of my appalled muſe
Foreweryed with the trauayle of my brayne
In ſcannyng of the argued Bookes diffuſe,
And darke for me the glimeryng ſyght
to gayne,
Debated lóng what exerſyce to vſe,
To fyle the edgeles partes of Wit agayne
To clenſe the Heade from ſleapy humours
ſlyme.
To rouſe the Hart from drowſye Dreames
in time.

The mind deſyres to brek from thoughtful denne
And time requyres the painted felds to vewe.
The Eye procures to pleaſe the Fancie then
With fieldiſh ſights of diuers colours newe.
The ſmelling likes the ſauour ſwete of them.
The Eare agrees the pleaſaunt laye anewe
Of Byrds to here. Thus theſe do all contryue,
With this diſporte the Spirits to reuyue.

But Fancie then, by ſerche of ſelfe deuyſe,
Renouncyng thus to ſpende the pleaſaunt Maye
So vainly out with ſport of fruteles Pryce
Found out at length, this practyſe for my playe,
To penne in Verſe, the toyes of her deuiſe,
To pas this tyme of Pentecoſte awaye
Whoſe ydle dayes, ſhe wyld me thus to ſpende.
And publiſh forth her doings in the ende.

Quod Reaſon no, (and brake her tale begon,
Wilt thou preſume, lyke Bayarde blynd to preſſe,
Into the throng of all the lookers on
Whoſe vewyng eyes, will wey thy wiſdom leſſe.

To ſe the threde of all thy workes yll ſpon
Drawen out at length, vnto the comon geſſe,
Then if thou ſhuldſt keepe to thy ſelfe thy clewe
Where none thy works beſydes thy ſelf may vew

With this roſe vp, from oute her Seate behynde,
Dame Memorye, and Reaſon thus beſought.
Since Lady chiefe of vs thou art aſſygnde
To rule and temper all my ſecrete thought
And to reſtrane affections Fancie blynde,
Let me entreate if I may perce the ought,
For to preſent a Solace very fytte
Our Sences dull with chaunged Muſe to whet,

Lo here the Eye a Paper buntche doth ſe
Of fyled worke of Googes flowing Heade,
Lefte here behynde, when hence he paſt from me,
In all the ſtormes that Winter blaſtes beſpreade
Through ſwellyng Seas and loftye mountains hye
Of Pyrenei the pathes vnknowen to treade.
Whoſe great good wyll I kepe, and in his place
His Verſes craue to repreſent his face.

Vnfolde the truſſe therfore and yf the Muſe
Be ſotted ſo with this graue Study paſt
In ſo ſhort ſpace, or if we ſeke to chuſe
To prynt our actes in ſafetie at the laſt
Ceaſe of a whyle this Labor and peruſe
Theſe Papers left of ſuche delyghting taſte
And put in prynt theſe workes of worthy Skyll
So ſhall we ſhowe the fruytes of our good wyll.

This Fancie lykte, imagynyng aryght
Of her owne Ioye in hearyng of his Verſe
And pleaſaunt Style, moſt pythyly endyght
whoſe Fame forth blowen, his deds could wel reherſe
But for to paynt my name in open ſight
with others Stuffe, this wold ſhe ſayne reuerſe,
And thinkes I ſhould in others Plumes ſo ſhow
My ſelfe, to be a ſeconde Eſops Crowe.

But after when the Eye had vewed eche Lyne.
That Googe had pend and left behynde with me,
when Memorye could all the effect refygne,
To Reafons Skyll, to weye them as they lye.
with long reherfe of tryed Fayth by tyme
Then Fancie foone her Pryde, began to plye
And all receyued muche pleafure to the Mynde
More profytte farre then Fancye had affygnde.

And Fancie thus her felfe with blufhyng face,
Condemned by Dame Reafons dome deuyne
To fe th[e]alluryng Style the cumly grace,
The fappye Sence of this his paffyng Ryme,
So farre furmountynge her Inuention bafe,
And hearyng of his frendlynes in fyne
whiche Memorye her Storehoufe held full fafte
Allowed well theyr Iudgements at the lafte.

Since euerye Sence did wonted ftrength renue,
The Blud congeld, recourfed to his place
The wyts benomd brought to their proper quue
The Hart oppreft with old delighting grace,
Vnburdend nowe and puft with pleafure newe
By takyng of this Booke the vewyng gafe.
They all at ons Good wyll nowe calde vpon,
To wreft her felfe to quyght thefe works anon.

Thus pufhte I forth ftrayghte to the Printers hande
Thefe Eglogs, Sonets, Epytaphes of men
Vnto the Readers Eyes for to be fkande,
with Prayfes fuche as is due vnto them
who abfent nowe theyr Mafter may commende,
And feade his Fame what foeuer fayleth him,
Gyue Googe therfore his owne deferued Fame,
Giue Blundefton leaue to wyfh wel to his name :

¶ *Finis.*

Egloga prima.

Daphnes. **Amintas.**

SYth *Phebus* now begins to flame,
O frende *Amintas* deare:
And placed hath his gorgeous *globe*
in midſte of all the Spheare
And from ye place doth caſt his Beames,
where (they that ſtarres deſyne)
Lyes poynt (doo ſaye) that termed is,
ryght Equinoctial lyne.
wheras the Ram doth cauſe to ſpring,
eche herbe and floure in fyelde
And forceth ground (yat ſpoyld of grene
Did lye,) newe grene to yelde.
Let ſhepherds vs yelde alſo tales,
as beſt becommes the tyme:
Such tales as Winter ſtormes haue ſtayde
in countrey Poets Ryme.
Begyn to ſynge *Amintas* thou,
for why? thy wyt is beſt:
And many a ſaged ſawe lies hyd
within thine aged breſt.
Ofte haue I heard, of Shephards old,
thy fame reported true,
No Herdman liues: but knowes the praiſe,
to olde *Amintas* due:
Begyn therfore, and I gyue eare,
for talke doth me delyght,
Go Boye: go dryue the Beaſtes to ſede
whyle he his mynde reſyght.

Amin. Thy prayſes *Daphnes* are to great,
and more for me than meete:
Nor euer I, ſuche ſaged ſawes,
could ſynge in Verſes ſweete.
And now, to talke of ſpring time tales
my heares to hoare, do growe,
Suche tales as theſe, I tolde in tyme,
when youthfull yeares dyd flowe.
But ſynce, I can not the denye,
thy Fathers loue doth bynde:
In ſymple Songe I wyll adreſſe
my ſelfe, to ſhowe my minde.
Longe haſt thou *Daphnes* me requyred
the ſtate of Loue to tell,
For in my youth, I knewe the force,
and paſſions all, full well.
Nowe Loue therfore I wyll define,
and what it is declare,
which way poore ſouls it doth entrap
and howe it them doth ſnare.
My Boie, remoue my beaſts from hens
and dryue them farther downe,
Vpon the Hylles, let them go feade,
that ioyne to yender towne,
O Cupyde kynge of fyerye Loue,
ayde thou my ſyngynge Verſe,
And teache me heare the cauſe and caſe,
Of Louers to reherſe,
Direct my tong, in trothe to treade,
with Furye fyll my brayne,
That I may able be to tell,
the cauſe of Louers payne.
Opinions diuers coulde I ſhowe,
but chiefeſt of them all,
I wyll declare: and for the reſt,
with ſilence leaue I ſhall.
A feruent Humour, (ſome do iudge)
within the Head doth lye,

Which yſſuyng forth with poyſoned beames
 doth ron from eye to eye :
And taking place abrode in heads,
 a whyle doth fyrmely reſt :
Till Phrenſie framde in Fancie fond,
 diſcends from hed, to breſt.
Plato. And poiſon ſtrong, from eies outdrawn
 doth perce the wretched harte,
And all infectes the bloud aboute,
 and boyles in euery parte:
Thus: when the beames, infected hath,
 the wofull Louers blud:
Then Sences al, do ſtrayght decaye,
 oppreſt with Furyes flud.
Then Lybertie withdrawes her ſelf,
 and Bondage beares the ſwaye,
Affection blynd then leades the hart,
 and Wyt, is wownde awaye.
O *Daphnes* then, the paines appeare,
 and tormentes all of hell.
Then ſekes, the ſelye wounded ſoule,
 the flames for to expell.
But all to late, alas he ſtryues,
 for Fancie beares the ſtroke
And he, muſt toyle (no helpe there is)
 in ſlauyſſhe ſeruyle yoke.
His blud corrupted all within,
 doth boyle in euery vayne,
Than ſekes he howe to ſewe for ſalue
 that maye redreſſe his payne.
And when the face, he doth beholde
 by whiche he ſhulde haue ayde,
And ſees no helpe, then lookes he long,
 and trembleth all afrayde.
And muſeth at the framed ſhape,
 that hath his lyfe in handes:
Nowe faſt he flies, aboute the flames,
 nowe ſtyll amaſed ſtandes:

Yet Hope relieues, his hurtful Heate
and Wyll doth Payne make lyght,
And al the griefes, that then he feeles
doth Presence styll requyght.
But when the Lyght absented is,
and Beames in hart remayne,
Then flames the Fyre fresh agayne,
and newe begyns his Payne.
Then longe he lookes, his losse to se,
then sobbes, and syghes abounde,
Then mourneth he, to mys the marke
that erst to soone he founde.
Then shadefull places oute he lookes,
and all alone he lyues,
Exylynge Ioye, and myrth from him,
hymselfe to waylynge gyues,
And styll his minde theron doth muse
and styll, therof he prates,
O *Daphnes* here I swere to the,
no griefe to Louers state.
Yf he but ones beholde the place,
where he was wont to mete,
The pleasaunt forme yat hym enflamd,
and ioyfull Countnaunce swete.
The place (a wonderous thing I tell)
his gryefe augmenteth newe,
Yet styll he sekes the place to se,
that moste he shulde eschewe.
Yf but the name rehearsed be
(a thynge more straunge to heare)
Then Colour commes and goes in hast
then quaketh he for feare,
The verye name, hath such a force,
that it can dase the mynde,
And make the man amasde to stande,
what force hath Loue to bynde?
Affection none to this is lyke,
it doth surmownt them all,

Of greiffes, the greateſt greif no doubt
 is to be *Venus* thrall,
And therfore, *Daphnes* nowe beware,
 for thou art yonge, and fre,
Take heade of vewynge faces longe,
 for loſſe of Lybertye,
I ſhall not nede (I thynke) to byd
 the, to deteſt the Cryme,
Iupiter. Of wycked loue, that *Ioue* did vſe,
 In *Ganimedes* tyme,
For rather wolde I (thoo it be muche)
 that thou ſhuldeſt ſeake the fyre,
Of lawfull Loue, that I haue tolde,
 than burne wyth ſuche deſyre,
And thus an end, I weryed am,
 my wynde is olde, and faynt,
Suche matters I, do leaue to ſuche,
 as finer farre can paint,
Fetche in the Gote: that goes aſtraye,
 and dryue hym to the folde,
My yeares be great I wyl be gone,
 for ſpryngtyme nyghts be colde.
Daphnes. Great thankes to the, for this thy tale,
 Amintas here I gyue:
But neuer can I make amendes
 to the whilſte I do lyue.
Yet for thy paynes (no recompence)
 a ſmall rewarde haue here.
A whiſtle framed longe ago,
 wherwith my father deare
His ioyfull beaſts, was wont to kepe.
 No Pype for tune ſo ſwete
Might ſhepharde euer yet poſſes.
 (a thynge for the full mete.)

Finis Eglogæ primæ.

Egloga ſecunda.

Dametas.

MY beaſts, go fede vpon ye plaine,
and let your herdman lye,
Thou ſeeſt her mind, and fearſt you nowe,
Dametas for to dye?
Why ſtayeſt you thus? why doſt you ſtay
thy lyſe to longe doth laſte:
Accounte this flud, thy fatall graue,
ſyth time of hope is paſte.
What meanſt thou thus to linger on?
thy life wolde fayne departe,
Alas: the wounde doth feſter ſtyll,
of curſed Cupids darte.
No ſalue but this, can helpe thy ſore,
no thynge can moue her minde
She hath decreed, that thou ſhalt dye,
no helpe there is to finde.
Nowe ſyth there is, no other helpe,
nor ought but this to trye,
Thou ſeeſt her mind: why fearſte thou than?
Dametas for to dye.
Long haſt thou ſerued, and ſerued true,
but all alas, in vayne,
For ſhe thy ſeruyce, nought eſtemes,
but deales the griefe for gayne.
For thy good wyll, (a gaye rewarde)
Diſdayne, for Loue ſhe gyues,
Thou loueſt her while thy life doth laſt,
ſhe hates the, w[h]ile ſhe liues.
Thou flamſte, when as you ſeeſt her face
with Heate of hye deſyre,
She flames agayne, but how? (alas)
with depe diſdaynfull Ire.
The greateſt pleaſure is to the,
to ſe her voyde of Payne,

The greatest gryefe to her agayne,
to se thy Health remayne.
Thou couetste euer her to fynde,
she sekes from the to flye,
Thou seest her mynd, why fearst thou than?
Dametas for to dye?
Doste thou accounte it best to kepe,
thy lyfe in sorrowes styll?
Or thynkste thou best it now to lyue,
Contrarye to her wyll?
Thynkste thou thy lyfe for to retaine?
when she is not content,
Canste thou addicte: thy selfe to lyue?
and she to murder bent.
Doste thou entende agayne, to sewe
for mercye at her handes?
As soone thou mayst go plow ye rocks,
and reape vpon the Sandes.
Draw nere O mighty Herd of beasts
syth no man els is bye,
Your Herdman longe that hathe you kept,
Dametas now must dye.
Resolue your Brutisshe eies to teares
and all togyther crye,
Bewayle the wofull ende of Loue,
Dametas nowe must dye.
My pleasaunt Songs, nowe shall you here
no more on Mountaines hye,
I leaue you all, I must be gone.
Dametas nowe must dye:
To *Titirus* I you resyne,
in Pasture good to lye,
For *Titirus* shall kepe you thoughe,
Dametas nowe must dye.
O cursed Cause, that hath me slayne,
My trothe alas to trye,
O Shephardes all, be Wytnesses,
Dametas here doth dye.

Finis Eglogæ secundæ.

Egloga tertia.

Menalcas. **Coridon.**

A Pleaſaunt wether *Coridon*,
and ſytte to kepe the ſyelde,
This moone hath brought, hearſt you the birds
what ioyfull tunes they yeld?
Loe: how the luſtie lambes do courſe,
whom ſpring time heate doth pricke
Beholde againe, the aged Yewes,
with bouncinge leapes do kicke,
Amon[g]ſt them all, what ayles thy ramme,
to halte ſo muche behynde,
Some ſore miſchaunce, hath him befaln
or els ſome griefe of minde,
For wonte he was, of ſtomacke ſtoute
and courage hye to be,
And looked proude, amongſt ye flocke,
and none ſo ſtout as he.

Cor. A great miſhap, and griefe of mynde,
is him befalne of late,
Which cauſeth him, againſt his wyll,
to loſe his olde eſtate.
A luſtie flocke hath *Titirus*,
that him *Dametas* gaue,
Dametas he, that Martir died,
whoſe ſoule the heaue[n]s haue,
And in this flocke, full many Yewes
of pleaſaunte forme do goe,
with them a mighty Ramme doth ronne,
that workes all Woers woe.
My Ramme, when he the pleaſaunt dames.
had vewed rounde aboute,

Chofe grounde of battayle, with his foe
and thought to fyght it oute.
But all to weake, (alas) he was,
althoughe his harte was good,
For when his enemye him efpied,
he ranne with cruell moode.
And with his croked weapon fmote,
hym fore vpon the fyde,
A blowe of force, that ftayde not there
but to the legges dyd glyde.
And almofte laamd the woer quyte.
(fuche happes in loue there be :)
This is the caufe, of all his griefe
and waylynge that you fe.

Men. Well *Coridon* let hym go halte,
and let vs both go lye,
In yonder buffhe of Iuniper,
the Beafts fhall fede hereby.
A pleafaunt place here is to talke:
good *Coridon* begyn,
And let vs knowe the Townes eftate,
that thou remaynest in.

Cor. The Townes eftate? *Menalcas* oh
thou makfte my harte to grone,
For Vice hath euery place poffefte,
and Vertue thence is flowne.
Pryde beares her felfe, as Goddeffe chiefe
and boaftes aboue ye Skye,
And Lowlynes an abiecte lyes,
with Gentlenes her bye,
Wyt is not ioynde with Symplenes,
as fhe was wont to be,
But fekes the ayde of Arrogance,
and craftye Polycie.
Nobylitie begyns to fade,
and Carters vp do fprynge,
Then whiche, no greater plague can hap,
nor more pernicious thynge.

Menalcas I haue knowen my ſelfe,
within this thyrtye yeare,
Of Lordes and Auncient Gentelmen
a hundreth dwellynge theare,
Of whom we Shephardes had reliefe
ſuche Gentlenes of mynde,
Was placed in theyr noble Hartes,
as none is nowe to fynde.
But Hawtynes and proude Diſdayne
hath nowe the chiefe Eſtate,
For ſyr Iohn Straw, and ſyr Iohn Cur,
wyll not degenerate.
And yet, they dare account them ſelues
to be of Noble bludde.
But Fiſſhe bred vp, in durtye Pooles,
wyll euer ſtynke of mudde.
I promyſe the *Menalcas* here,
I wolde not them enuye.
Yf any ſpot of Gentlenes
in them I myght eſpye.
For yf theyr Natures gentell be,
thoughe byrth be neuer ſo baſe,
Of Gentelmen (for mete it is)
they ought haue name and place:
But when by byrth, they baſe are bred,
and churliſſhe harte retaine,
Though place of gentlemen thei haue
yet churles they do remayne.
A prouerbe olde, hath ofte ben harde
and now full true is tryed:
An Ape, wyll euer be an Ape,
thoughe purple garments hyde.
For ſeldom, wyll the maſtye courſe,
the Hare or els the Deare:
But ſtyll, accordynge to his kynde.
wyll holde, the hogge by th[e]eare.
Vnfitte are dunghill knights to ſerue
the towne, with Speare in fielde:

Nor ſtrange it ſemes, (a sudain Chop)
to leape from whyp, to ſhielde.
The chiefeſt man, in all our towne,
that beares the greateſt ſwaye,
Is *Coridon* no kynne to me,
a Neteherd th[e]other daye.
This *Coridon* come from the Carte,
In honour chiefe doth ſytte,
And gouernes vs: becauſe he hath
a Crabbed, Clowniſh wytte.
Nowe ſe the Churlyſh Crueltye,
that in hys harte remayns.
The ſelye Sheape yat Shephards good,
haue foſterd vp wyth Paynes,
And browght awaye, from Stynkyng dales
on pleaſant Hylles to feade:
O Cruell Clowniſh Coridon
O curſed Carliſh Seade:
The ſimple Shepe, conſtrayned he,
theyr Paſture ſwete to leaue,
And to theyr old corrupted Graſſe,
enforceth them to cleaue.
Such Shepe, as would not them obaye
but in theyr Paſture byde,
with (cruell flames,) they did conſume
and vex on euery ſyde.
And with the ſhepe, ye Shephardes good,
(O hate full Hounds of Hell,)
They did torment, and dryue them out,
in Places farre to dwell.
There dyed *Daphnes* for his Shepe,
the chiefeſt of them all.
And fayre *Alexis* flamde in Fyre,
who neuer peryſhe ſhall.
O Shephards wayle, for *Daphnes* deth,
Alexis hap lament,
And curs the force of cruell hartes,
that them to death haue ſent.

I, ſynce I ſawe ſuche ſynfull ſyghts,
dyd neuer lyke the Towne,
But thought it beſt to take my ſheepe,
and dwell vpon the downe.
Wheras I lyue, a pleaſaunt lyfe,
and free from cruell handes,
I wolde not leaue, the pleaſaunt fyelde
for all the Townyſh Landes.
For ſyth that Pryde, is placed thus,
and Vice ſet vp ſo hye:
And Crueltie doth rage ſo ſore,
and men lyue all awrye:
Thynkſte you? yat God, will long forbere,
his ſcourge, and plague to ſende?
To ſuche as hym do ſtyll deſpyſe,
and neuer ſeke to mende?
Let them be ſure he wyll reuenge,
when they thynke leaſte vpon.
But looke a ſtormy ſhowre doth ryſe,
whiche wyll fall heare anone,
Menalcas beſt we nowe departe,
my Cottage vs ſhall keepe,
For there is rowme for the, and me,
and eke for all our ſheepe:
Som Cheſtnuts haue I there in ſtore
with Cheeſe and pleaſaunt whaye,
God ſends me Vittayles for my nede,
and I ſynge Care awaye.

¶ *Finis Eglogæ tertiæ.*

Egloga quarta.

Melibeus. Palemon.

O God, that guyds ye golden *Globe*,
wher ſhinyng ſhapes do dwel
O thou yat throweſt the thunder thumps
from Heauens hye, to Hell,
what wonders workes thy worthynes
what meruayles doſte thou frame?
What ſecrete ſyghts be Subiect ſene
vnto thy holy name?
A ſymple Shepharde ſlayne of late,
by foolyſhe force of Loue,
That had not Grace ſuch fancies fond
and Flames for to remoue,
Appeared late, before myne eies,
(Alas I feare to ſpeake,)
Not as he here was wont to lyue,
whyle Gryefe hym none did breake.
But all in Blacke, he clothed came
an vgly ſyght to ſe:
As they that for theyr due Deſartes,
with Paynes tormented be,
My ſhepe for feare amaſed ran,
and fled from Hyll to Dale,
And I alone remayned there,
with countenaunce wan and pale.
O Lorde (quoth I) what meanes this thyng
is this *Alexis* ſpryght?
Or is it *Daphnes* ſoule that ſhowes?
to me this dredfull ſyght,
Or comes ſome Feend of Hell abrode?
with feare men to torment?
Megera this? or *Tiſiphon*?
Or is *Alecto* ſent?

what ſoeuer thou art, yat thou doſt com?
  Ghooſt, Hagge, or Fende of Hell:
I the commaunde by hym that lyues,
  thy name and caſe to tell.
With this, a stynkyng ſmoke I ſawe,
  from out his mouth to flye,
And with that ſame, his voyce did ſound,
  None of them all am I.
But ons thy frende (*O Melibei*)
  Dametas was my name,
Dametas I, that ſlewe my ſelfe,
  by force of foolyſſhe flame.
Dametas I, that dotynge dyed,
  In fyre of vnkynde Loue:
Dametas I, whom *Deiopey*
  dyd cauſe ſuche ende to proue,
The ſame *Dametas* here I com,
  by lycens vnto the:
For to declare the wofull ſtate,
  that happens now to me.
(*O Melibei*) take hede of Loue,
  of me Example take,
That ſlewe my ſelfe, and liue in Hell,
  for *Deiopeias* ſake.
I thought that Deth ſhuld me releaſe
  from paynes and dolefull woe,
But nowe (alas) the trothe is tryed,
  I fynde it nothynge ſoe,
For looke what Payne and gryefe I felt
  when I lyued heare afore:
With thoſe I nowe tormented am,
  and with ten thouſand more.
I meane not that I burne in loue,
  ſuche foolyſh toyes begon,
But Gryefes in nombre haue I lyke
  and manye more vpon.
O curſed Loue, (what ſhulde I ſaye,)
  that brought me fyrſte to Payne,

Well, myght I ones despyse thy lore,
but nowe (alas) in vayne.
With fond Affection, I dyd flame,
whiche nowe I moste repent,
But all to late (alas) I wayle,
syth hope of Grace is spent.
The fickle fadynge forme, and face,
that ones so muche I sowght,
Hath made me lose the Skyes aboue,
and me to Hell hath browght.
Why had I Reason delt to me?
and coulde not Reason vse.
Why gaue I Brydle to my wyll?
when I myght well refuse.
A wycked Wyll, in dede it was,
that blynded so my syght,
That made me on such fadyng Duste,
to set my whole Delyght,
A fonde Affection lead me then,
When I for God dyd place,
A Creature, cause of all my Care,
a flesshye fletynge face,
A woman Waue of Wretchednes,
a Paterne pylde of Pryde,
A Mate of Myschiefe and Distresse,
for whom (a Foole) I dyed.
Thus whyle he spake, I sawe me thought
of Hell an vglye Fende,
With lothsome Clawes, hym for to close
and forced him there to ende.
And with this same, (O *Melibey*,)
farewell, farewell, (quoth he)
Eschewe the Blase of feruent flames,
Example take of me.
My Harte with this began to rent,
and all amasde I stoode.
O lord (quoth I) what flames be these
what Rage, what Furyes woode?

Doth Loue procure, to wretched men
  what Bondage doth it brynge?
Paine here: and Payne in life to come.
  (O dolefull, dredefull thynge.)
[Palemon] I quake to heare, this Storye tolde,
  and *Melibei* I fainte,
For ſure I thought *Dametas* had,
  been placed lyke a Saynte.
I thought that cruel *Charons* Boate,
  had myſte of hym her frayght.
And through his deth, he mounted had
  to ſtarres and Heauens ſtrayght.
Howe valiantly dyd he deſpyſe,
  his lyfe in Bondage ledde?
And ſekyng Deth with courage hye,
  from Loue and Ladye fledde.
And is he thus rewarded nowe?
  The ground be curſed than,
That foſterde vp, ſo fayre a face
  that loſte ſo good a Man.

¶ *Finis Eglogæ quartæ.*

Egloga quinta.

Mopsus. Egon.

SOm doleful thing there is at hand
thy countenaunce doth declare,
Thy face good *Egon* voide of blud
thine eies amaſed ſtare:
I ſe thy teares, howe they do ſtill,
diſcloſe thy ſecrete mynde,
Hath Fortune frowned late on the?
Hath Cupide ben vnkinde.

Egon. A pyteous thingé to be bewalyde
a deſperate Acte of Loue,
(O Deſtenies) ſuche cruell broyles
How haue you power to moue?
Here lyued a Ladye fayre of late,
that *Claudia* men dyd call:
Of goodly forme, yea ſuche a one,
as farre ſurmounted all.
The ſtately Dames, yat in this Courte,
to ſhowe them ſelues do lye,
There was not one in all the Crewe:
that could come Claudia nye.
A worthy Knyght dyd loue her longe,
and for her ſake did ſeale.
The panges of Loue, that happen ſtyl
by frownyng Fortunes wheale,
He had a Page, *Valerius* named,
whom ſo muche he dyd truſte,
That all the ſecrets of his Hart,
to hym declare he muſte.
And made hym all the onely meanes,
to ſue for his redreſſe,
And to entreate for grace to her,
that cauſed his diſtreſſe.

She whan as fyrſt ſhe ſaw his page
was ſtrayght with hym in Loue,
That nothynge could *Valerius* face,
from *Claudias* mynde remoue.
By hym was *Fauſtus* often harde,
by hym his ſutes toke place,
By hym he often dyd aſpyre,
to ſe his Ladyes face.
This paſſed well, tyll at the length,
Valerius ſore dyd ſewe,
With many teares beſechynge her,
his Mayſters gryefe to rewe.
And tolde her that yf ſhe wolde not
releaſe, his Mayſters payne,
He neuer wolde attempte her more,
nor ſe her ones agayne.
She then with maſed countnaunce there
and teares yat guſhing fell,
Aſtonyed anſwerde thus, loe nowe,
alas I ſe to well.
Howe longe I haue deceyued ben,
by the *Valerius* heare,
I neuer yet beleued before,
nor tyll this tyme dyd feare,
That thou dydſte for thy Mayſter ſue
but onely for my ſake.
And for my ſyght, I euer thought,
thou dydſte thy trauayle take.
But nowe I ſe the contrarye,
thou nothynge carſte for me,
Synce fyrſt thou knewſte, the fyerye flames
that I haue felte by the.
O Lorde howe yll, thou doſte requyte
that I for the haue done,
I curſe the time, that frendſhyp fyrſt,
to ſhowe, I haue begon.
O lorde I the beſeche let me,
in tyme reuenged be:

And let hym knowe that he hate ſynd,
in this miſuſynge me,
I can not thynke, but Fortune once,
ſhall the rewarde for all,
And vengeaunce due for thy deſerts,
in tyme ſhall on the fall.
And tell thy maiſter *Fauſtus* nowe,
yf he wolde haue me lyue:
That neuer more he ſewe to me,
this aunſwere laſte I gyue:
And thou o Traytour vyle,
and enmye to my lyfe,
Abſent thy ſelfe from out my ſyght,
procure not greater ſtryſe,
Synce yat theſe teares, had neuer force
to moue thy ſtoneye harte,
Let neuer theſe my weryed eyes,
ſe the no more. Departe.
This ſayde, in haſte ſhe hieth in,
and there doth vengeaunce call,
And ſtrake her ſelf, with cruel knyfe,
and bluddye downe doth fall.
This dolfull chaunce, whan *Fauſtus* heard
lamentynge lowde he cryes,
And teares his heare and doth accuſe,
the vniuſt and cruell Skies.
And in this ragynge moode awaye,
he ſtealeth oute alone,
And gone he is: no man knowes where
eche man doth for hym mone.
Valerius whan he doth perceyue,
his Mayſter to be gone:
He weepes and wailes, in piteous plight
and forth he ronnes anone.
No Man knowes where, he is becom,
ſome ſaye the wooddes he tooke,

Intendynge there to ende his lyfe,
on no Man more to looke :
The Courte lamentes, the Princeſſe eke
her ſelfe doth weepe for woe,
Loe, *Fauſtus* fled, and *Claudia* deade.
Valerius vanyſſhed too.

¶ *Finis Eglogæ quintæ.*

Egloga sexta.

Felix. Faustus.

Felix. O *Faustus*, whom aboue the reſt,
of Shephardes here that kepe,
Vpon theſe holts, ye nombre great
of waightye fleeſed ſhepe:
I euer haue eſtemde: and counted eke,
the chiefeſt Frende of all,
What great miſhap, what ſcourge of minde
or griefe hath the befall?
That hath the brought in ſuch a plight
farre from thy wonted guyſe?
What meanes this countenaunce all beſprent
with teres? theſe wretched eies
This mournynge looke, this Veſture ſad
this wrethe of Wyllow tree,
(Vnhappy man) why doſte thou wepe
what chaunce hath altered the?
Tell tell, me ſoone, I am thy frende,
Diſcloſe to me thy gryeſe,
Be not afrayde, for frendes do ſerue,
to gyue theyr Frendes relyeſe.

Faustus. The woſull cauſe of all my hurte,
good *Felix* longe agoe,
Thou knewſt full well: I nede not now
by wordes to double woe,
Synce that (alas) all hope is paſt
ſynce gryefe, and I am one,
And ſynce the Ladye of my lyſe,
(my faute) I haue forgone,
What woldſt you haue me do (oh frend?)
to Ioye? in ſuch dyſtres?

Naye pleasures quyte I banish here,
and yelde to Heuynes,
Let gryefes torment me euermore,
let neuer Cares awaye.
Let neuer Fortune turne her wheale
to gyue me blysfull daye.
Loue hath me scourged: I am content
lament not thou my state,
Let spyght on me take vengeaunce nowe
let me be torne with hate.
Let her enioye, her happye lyfe,
a Flowre of golden hewe,
A Mary-golde. That closeth when the Son doth set,
and spreads with Phebus newe.
Syth from my Garlande now is falne,
this famouse Flowre swete:
Let Wyllows wynde aboute my hed,
(a Wrethe for Wretches mete)
Felix. Fye *Faustus*, let not Fancie fonde,
in the beare suche a swaye,
Expell Affections from thy mynde,
and dryue them quyght awaye.
Embrace thine Auncient Lybertie,
let Bondage vyle be fled:
Let Reason rule, thy crased Brayne,
place Wyt, in Folies steade.
Synce she is gone, what remedye?
why shuldest thou so lament?
Wilt thou destroy thy self with tears
and she to pleasures bent?
Gyue eare to me, and I wyll showe
the remedies for Loue
That I haue learned longe agoe:
and in my youth dyd proue.
Such remedies as soone shall quenche
the flames of Cupids Fyre,
Suche remedies as shall delaye,
the Rage of fonde Desyre.

For *Fauſtus* yf thou folow ſtyll,
the blynded God to pleaſe,
And wylt not ſeke, by Reaſons Rule,
to purchaſe thyne owne eaſe,
Long canſt thou not thy frends enioy
but byd them all farewell.
And leaue thy lyfe, and giue thy ſoule
to depeſt fluds of Hell.
Leaue of therfore, betymes and let
Affection beare no ſwaye,
And now at fyrſt the Fyre quench
before it further ſtraye,
Eche thyng is eaſely made to obaye,
whyle it is yong and grene,
The tender twyg, that now doth bend
at length refuſeth cleane.
The feruent Fyre, that flamyng fyrſt,
may lytell water drenche,
When as it hath obtayned tyme,
whole Ryuers can not quenche:
Forſake the Town, (my *Fauſtus* deare)
and dwell, vpon this playne,
And tyme ſhall heale, thy feſtryng wound
and Abſence banyſh Payne.
Aboue all thynges fly Idlenes,
For this doth dowble ſtrength,
To Louers flams, and makes them rage,
tyl all be loſt at length,
Here in thes felds, are pleaſaunt things
to occupye thy brayn,
Be hold: how ſpryng reuyues agayn,
that winter late had ſlayne,
Behold: the pleſaunt Hylles adournd,
with dyuers colours fayre,
Geue eare to *Scillas* luſty ſonges,
reioyſynge in the ayr,
What pleaſure canſt thou more deſyre,
then here is for to ſe:

Thy lufty yewes, with many a lam,
  Lo: whear they wayt on the,
Thynke not vpon that curfed face,
  that makes the thus her flaue
But well regard the pleafaunt lyfe,
  that here thou feeft me haue,
Whan I long tyme a go, did feale,
  the flames of *Cupids* fyre,
Thefe meanes Lo thou I practifed,
  to cure my fond defyre.
I fyrft wayed with my felfe,
  How fond a thyng it feamd,
To let my heart lye there in chaynes,
  where I was nought efteamd.
And how with flames I burnt for her,
  that paffed nought for me,
And how, thefe eyes encreaft my harmes
  that fyrft her face did fe,
With penfyfe heart full fraight with thoughts,
  I fled from thence away,
And though that Loue bad tourne my fteppes.
  yet wold I neuer ftay,
But from that foule infectyue ayer,
  wher firft I tooke my fore,
I hyed in haft, and fhund the place,
  to fe for euer more.
Eache letter that I had receyued
  from her, I caft away,
And tokens all, I threw them down,
  to my no fmall dyfmay.
Then bufyed I my felfe in thyngs
  that myght me mofte delyght,
And fought the chiefft means I could,
  to helpe my weryed fpryght.
Somtyme I wold behold the fyelds,
  and Hylles that thou dofte fe,
Somtime I wold betraye the Byrds,
  that lyght on lymed tree,
Efpecially in Shepftare tyme,
  when thicke in flockes they flye,

One wold I take, and to her Leg,
a lymed Lyne wold tye,
And where ye flock flew thickeſt, there
I wold her caſt awaye,
She ſtrayght vnto the reſt wold hye,
amongſt her Mates to playe.
And preaſyng in the mydſte of them,
with Lyne and Lyme, and all,
With cleuyng wyngs, entangled faſt.
they downe togyther fall.
Somtyme I wold the lytel Fyſh:
with bayted Hooke beguyle :
Somtyme the craftye Foxe I wold,
deceyue for all his wyle:
Somtyme the Wolfe, I wold purſue,
ſomtyme the ſomyng Boore :
And whan with labour all the daye,
my weryed Lyms were ſoore.
Than reſt and ſlepe I ſtraightway ſought
no Dreames dyd me afraye :
Tormented nought with care, I paſt
the lyngryng nyght awaye.
And thus I cleane forgot : in tyme,
the dotyng Dayes I ſawe,
And freed my ſelf, to my great Ioye,
from Yoke of Louers Lawe.
More of this ſame, I wyll the tell,
the next tyme here we mete,
And ſtronger Medycines wyll I gyue,
to purge that Venym ſwete.
Beholde the Daye is ſlypt awaye,
and Starres do faſt appeare.
Loe where *Caliſto* Virgin ones.
doth ſhyne in Skies ſo cleare.
Loe where olde *Cepheus* walks about,
with twynyng Serpent bye,
We wyll no lenger heare abyde.
But hence wyll homwarde hye.

Finis Eglogæ ſextæ.

Egloga septima.

Siluanus. **Sirenus.** **Seluagia.**

S*Irenus* ſhephard good and thou,
  that haſt yll lucke in loue,
The cauſe of al my hurt by whom
  my ſutes could neuer proue.
God neuer let that I ſhuld ſeeke,
  to be reuenged of the,
For whan I might haue ben with eaſe,
  yet wold not ſuffer me
The Loue that I, *Diana* bare,
  on the to ſhowe my Spyte :
On the in whom my Ladye fayre,
  had once her whole delyght,
If thy myſhaps do not me greue,
  My miſchieefs neuer ende.
Thynke not *ſirenus* that bycauſe,
  Diana was thy frend,
I beare the worſer wyl aſſure thy ſelf
  ſo baſe my loue neuer ſemde
That onely I ſhuld fauour her.
  but all that ſhe eſtemde.

Siren. Thou eyther art *siluanus* borne,
  Example for to gyue,
To vs that know not how,
  whan Fortune frownes to lyue,
Or els hath Nature placed in the
  ſo ſtrong and ſtoute a mynde.
Suffyſynge not, thyne yls alone
  to beare, but meanes to ſynde,

In Mr. Huth's copy—though the signatures are regular—the first *two* pages of the final original impression down to, *she kyld a faythfull frende*, on the next page are omitted : being represented by a blank *page*. They have been supplied by the kindness of W. A. Wright, Esq., M.A., from the copy in the library of Trinity College, Cambridge

That may the Griefes of others help,
I ſe thou art ſo bent,
That Fortune can the not amaſe,
For all her myſciefes ment,
I promys the *ſiluanus* heare,
tyme playne in the doth ſhow,
How dayly ſhe diſcouers things,
that erſt dyd men not know.
I can not beare the Gryefes I feale,
my force is all to faynt,
I neuer could as thou canſt ſtynt,
the teares of my complaynt.
Diana hath procured the paynes,
that I ſhall neuer ende,
When fyrſt ſhe falſt her troth to me,
ſhe kyld a faythfull frende.

Siluan. I meruayle how ſhe could ſo ſoone,
put the out of her mind,
I well remembre ſynce thou wentſte
alone I dyd her ſynd.
In place that ſorow ſemde to ſhape,
where no man ſtood her nye,
But onely (I vnhappy wretche,)
that herd her wofull crye,
And this with teares alowde ſhe ſayd,
O wretche in yll tyme borne.
What chaunce haſt thou? that thus thou haſt
Sirenus ſwete forlorne.
Gyue ouer pleaſures now,
Let neuer Ioye the pleaſe,
Seke all the cruell meanes thou canſt
that may thy hart dyſeaſe.
Whan thou doſte hym forget I wyſh,
all miſchifes on the lyght,
And after death, the Fendes of Hell,
torment thy lyuyng ſpryght.

Siren. What man wold here beleue?
that ſhe that thus could ſpeake,

In so shorte tyme as I haue bene
  awaye, wolde promys breake.
O stedfastnes and Constancy,
  how seldome are you founde:
In womens harts to haue your seats,
  Or long abydyng ground?
Who looke how much more earnest they,
  at fyrst theyr hearts do set,
So much more sooner euer more,
  where late they loued, forget:
Full well could euer I beleue,
  all women gylty of this:
Saue her alone, in whom I iudge,
  neuer nature wrought amis:
But sins her maryage how she speeds
  Siluan I pray the tell?

Siluan. Some say she lykes it very ill,
  and I beleue it well:
For *Delius* he that hath her now,
  although he welthy be,
Is but a lout and hath in hym,
  no hansome qualytie:
For as for all, suche thynges wherin,
  we Shepeheardes haue delyght,
As in Quaiting, Leaping, Singing or
  to sound a Bagpype ryght:
In all these thinges he is but an Asse,
  and nothyng do he can,
They saye tys quallities but tush,
  Its ryches makes a man:

Siren. What woman is that yat commeth here,
  Siluan canst thou tell?

Siluan. Its one hath sped as well in Loue,
  as we, I knowe her well:
She is one of fayre *Dianas* frendes,
  who keeps her beasts below,
Not far from hence bi her thou maist
  Dianas State wel know.

She loued hear a Shephearde cald,
Alanius longe a go :
Who fauers one *ysmenia* now,
the cause of al her wo :

Siluag. No place so fyt for the as this,
Lo heare *Siluanus* stands,
Who hath receaued lyke luck to thine
at cruel Fortunes hands,
This company besemes the well,
Fayr Shepheards both good deane,

Siluan. To the *Seluagia* eke of Hope,
Whom Loue hath spoyled cleane :
A thousande better dayes I wysh,
than thou hast had before,

Seluag. At length may better Fortune fall,
For worse can not be more.
To truste the fayned words of men,
Loe, thus poore women speeds.

Siluan. And men do smarte not through your words
but your vnconstant deeds.
For you when earnestlyest you loue,
no thyng can chaunce so lyght.
But yf a toye com in your Brayne,
your mynde is altered quyght.
If we but ones, absent our selues,
the shortest tyme we maye,
So muche vnconstant is your minde
Loue foreth strayght awaye,
Example take *Sirenus* here
whom once *Diana* lovd,
As all we know, and looke how soone
her mynd is now removd :
No, no, there is not one of you,
that constant can remayne :

Siluag. You iudge but of malicious hart,
and of a Ialouse brayne.
All thyngs you do your selues esteme,
and men must beare no blame.

Of your diſſemblyng noughty deeds,
we women beare the ſhame.

Siren. Fayre Dameſell yf you can perceyue
Siluanus true doth ſaye
There is not one amongſt you all,
but doth from reaſon ſtraye.
What is the cauſe that women thus?
in theyr vnconſtancye,
Do caſt a man from hyeſt hap,
to deepeſt myſerye?
Its nothyng els, I you aſſure,
but that you know not well,
What thing is loue, and what you haue,
in hand you can not tell.
Your ſymple wyts are all to weake,
Vnfayned loue to know,
And therof doth forgetfulnes,
in you ſo ſhortly grow.

Seluag. *Sirenus* iudge not ſo of vs,
our wyts be not ſo baſe,
But that we know as well as you,
whats what in euery caſe.
And women eke, there are ynow
that could yf they were brought
Teache men to lyue, and more to loue,
yf loue myght well be tought,
And for all this, yet do I thynke,
No thyng can worſer be.
Than womens ſtate, it is the worſt,
I thynke of eche degree.
For yf they ſhow but gentle words
you thynke for loue they dye.
And yf they ſpeake not when you liſt,
than ſtrayght you ſay, they are hye.
And that they ar, diſdainfull Dames.
and if they chaunce to talke.
Than cownt you them for chatring Pies
whoſe tongs muſt alwayes walke.

And yf perhaps they do forbeare,
  and Sylence chaunce to keepe,
Than tush, she is not for company,
  she is but a symple sheepe.
And yf they beare good wyll to one,
  then straight they are iudged nought.
And yf yll name to shun they leaue,
  Vnconstant they are thought.
Who nowe can please these Ialouse heads,
  the faute is all in you,
For women neuer wold chaunge their minds
  yf men wold styll be true.

Siren. To this, I well could answere you,
  but tyme doth byd me staye,
And women must the last worde haue
  no man may say them naye.
Passe ouer this, and let vs here,
  what lucke you haue had in loue,
And showe yf euer loue of man,
  your constaunt hart could moue.
No fytter place can be than this,
  here maye you safely rest,
Thus sytting here, declare at large,
  the secretes of your brest.

Siluag. Naye: lenger here we maye not byde,
  but home we mvst awaye,
Loe how the Son denies his Beames
  depriuyng vs of daye.

Finis Eglogæ septimæ.

Egloga octaua.

Coridon. **Cornix.**

NOw ragethe *Titan* fyerce aboue
his Beames on earth do beate.
Whoſe hote reflection maks vs feale
an ouer feruent heate:
Wyth ſyery Dog, he forward flames
hote Agues vp he dryues:
And ſends them downe, with boylyng blud
to ſhorten Myſers lyues.
Loe, how the beaſts, lyes vnder trees
how all thyng ſeekes the ſhade,
O bleſſed God, that ſome defence,
for euery hurte haſt made,
Beholde this pleaſaunte Brodeleaued Beech
and ſpringing fountain cleare,
Heare ſhade ynough, here water cold
com *Cornix* reſt we here,
And let vs ſongs begyn to ſyng,
our purs and harts be lyght.
We fere not we, the tomblyng world
we breake no ſleaps by nyght.

Cornix. Both place and tyme my *Coridon*
exhorteth me to ſynge,
Not of the wretched Louers lyues,
but of the immortall kynge.
Who gyues vs paſture for our beaſts
and bleſſeth our encreaſe:
By whom, while other cark and toyle
we lyue at home with eaſe.
Who keepes vs down, from climyng hye
wher honour breeds debate,

And here hath graunted vs to lyue
  in ſymple Shephards ſtate,
A lyfe that ſure doth fare exceade,
  eche other kynd of lyfe:
O happy ſtate, that doth content,
  How farre be we from ſtryſe?
Of hym therſore, me lyſt to ſynge,
  and of no wanton toyes,
For hym to loue, and hym to prayſe,
  ſurmounts all other Ioyes.
O Shephards leaue *Cupidoes* Camp,
  the ende wherof is vyle,
Remoue Dame *Venus* from your eies
  and harken here a whyle.
A God there is, that guyds the Globe,
  and framde the ſyckle Spheare,
And placed hath, the Starres aboue,
  that we do gaſe on here,
By whom we lyue, (vnthankful beaſts)
  by whom we haue our health,
By whom we gayne our happy ſtates
  by whom we get our wealth.
A God: that ſends vs that we nede,
  a God: that vs defends.
A God: from whom the Angels hye,
  on mortall men attends.
A God: of ſuche a Clemencie,
  that who ſo hym doth loue
Shall here be ſure to reſt a whyle,
  and alwayes reſt aboue.
But we, for hym do lytell care,
  His Heaſts we nought eſteme,
But hunt for thyngs that he doth hate
  moſt pleaſaunt thoſe do ſeme,
(Vnthankfull myſers) what do we?
  what meane we thus to ſtraye?
From ſuche a God, ſo mercyfull,
  to walke a worſer waye?

Maye nought his benefyts procure?
  maye nought his mercyes moue?
Maye nothynge bynde, but nedes we muſt?
  gyue hate to hym for loue?
O happy (ten tymes) is the man,
  (a Byrde full rare to fynde)
That loueth God with all his hart,
  and kepes his lawes in mynde.
He ſhalbe bleſt in all his works,
  and ſafe in euery tyme,
He ſhall ſwete quietnes enioye,
  whyle other ſmarte for Cryme.
The threatnyng chaunces of the world
  ſhall neuer hym annoye.
When Fortune frowns on fooliſh men
  he ſhalbe ſure to ioye.
For why? the Aungels of the Lorde,
  ſhall hym defende alwayes,
And ſet hym free, at euery harmes,
  and hurts at all aſſayes.
Dauid. [? Daniel.] Euen he that kept the Prophet ſafe,
  from mouthes of Lyons wylde,
Moses. And he that once preſerued in Flags,
  the ſely ſuckyng Chylde,
Elias. The God that fed, by Rauens Byll,
  the Teacher of his worde,
Shall hym (no doubt) in ſafetie keepe,
  from Famyn, Fyre, aud Sworde.
Not he, whom Poets old haue faynd,
  to lyue in Heauen hye,
Iupiter. Embracyng Boyes: (O ſylthy thyng)
  in beaſtly Lecherye.
Iuno. Nor *Iuno* ſhe: (that wrinkled Iade,)
  that Quene of Skyes is calde,
Saturn. Nor ſoleyn *Saturn* Churlyſh Chuffe,
  with Scalpe of Cancre bald.
Mars. Nor ſumyng Foole, with ſyery face,
  that moues the ſyghters mynd.

Venus Nor Venus ſhe: (that wanton wench)
Cupid. that guyds the Shoter blynd.
Can the defende: as God wyll do,
for they were ſynfull fooles,
Homerus. Whom fyrſt ye blynd hye witted Greke
brought in to wyſe mens Scooles.
No none of theſe, but God alone,
ought worſhyp for to haue,
For they for all theyr Honour ones,
reſt yet in ſtynkyng Graue.
Heare haſt thou heard, the happy ſtate
of them that lyue in feare,
Of God: and loue hym beſt: now lyſt,
his foes reward to heare,
And fyrſt know thou that euery man,
that from this God doe goe,
And folows luſt, hym he acountes,
to be his deadly foe,
This myghty Kyng of whom we talk,
as he is mercyfull,
And ſuffers long, reuengyng ſlow,
So when we be thus dull,
That we wyl not perceaue in tyme,
the goodnes of his grace,
His fauour ſtraight, he doth withdraw
and tournes a way his face.
And to him ſelfe then doth he ſay,
How long ſhall I permit
Theſe ſtubburne beaſtes, for to rebell?
and ſhall I loue them yet,
That hate me thus? or haue I nede
theyr louynge mynds to craue?
I aſke no more but onely loue,
and that I can not haue.
Well, wel I wil not care for them,
that thus do me dyſpyſe,
Let them go lyue, euen as they lyſt,
I turne awaye myne eyes.

When God hath thus ſayd to him ſelf
  Then doth the braynleſſe foole,
Caſt Brydle of, and out he runnes,
  neglectynge vertues Scoole,
Then doth the Deuyl geue him lyne,
  and let him rune at large,
And Pleaſure makes his Mariner,
  to row in vyces Barge,
Then vp the Sayles of wilfulnes.
  he hoyſes hie in haſt,
And fond Affection blowes hym forth,
  a wynd that *Pluto* plaſt,
Then cuttes he ſwyſt, the ſeas of ſin,
  and through the Chanell deape,
With Ioyful mynd, he fleets a pace,
  whom Pleaſure bryngs a ſleape,
Then who ſo happy thinks hym ſelfe?
  who dreames of ioy but he?
Tuſh, tuſh, ſayeth he: to thynk of God,
  In age ſuffiſeth me.
Now wil I paſſe my pleaſaunt youth,
  Such toyes becomes this age,
And God ſhall followe me ſayth he,
  I wyll not be his page,
I wyll be prowd, and looke a loft,
  I wyll my bodye decke,
With coſtly clothes, a boue my ſtate
  who then dare gyue me checke?
Coridon. Garments ſom time, ſo gard a knaue,
  that he dare mate a Knyght,
Yet haue I ſene a *Nec* in hemp,
  For Checking often lyght.
Cornix. The Peacocks plume ſhal not me pas
  that nature finely framde
For coulord ſylkes ſhal ſet me fourth,
  that nature ſhalbe ſhamde,
My Sworde ſhal get me valiant fame,
  I wyll be *Mars* out ryght,

And *Mars* you know, muſt *Venus* haue,
  to recreate his ſpryght.
I wyll oppreſſe the ſymple knaue,
  ſhall Slaues be ſawſy now?
Nay: I wyll teache the nedy Dogges,
  with Cappe to crowche, and bow.
Thus fareth he, and thus he lyues,
  No whyt eſtymyng God,
In health, in ioy, and luſtynes,
  free from the ſmartyng Rod,
But in the midſt of all his myrth,
  whyle he ſuſpecteth leaſt,
His happy chaunce, begyns to chaunge
  and eke his fleetynge feaſt,
For death (that old deuouryng Wolf)
  whom goodmen nothyng feare,
Coms ſaylyng faſt, in Galley blacke,
  and whan he ſpyes hym neare,
Doth boorde hym ſtrayght, and grapels faſt
  And than begyns the fyght,
In ryot leapes, as Captayne chiefe,
  and from the Maynmaſt ryght,
He downward coms, and ſurfet than
  aſſayleth by and by,
Then vyle deſeaſes forward ſhoues,
  with paynes and gryefe therby,
Lyfe ſtands aloft, and fyghteth hard,
  but pleaſure all agaſte.
Doth leaue his ore, and out he flyes,
  then death approcheth faſt.
And giues the charge ſo ſore, yat needs
  muſt lyfe begyn to flye,
Then farewell all. The wretched man
  with Caryen Corſe doth lye,
Whom Deth hymſelf flyngs ouer bord,
  amyd the Seas of ſyn,
The place wher late, he ſwetly ſwam,
  now lyes he drowned in.

Contynuall torment hym awaytes,
(a Monſter vyle to tell)
That was begot of Due Deſert,
and raygneth now in Hell,
With gredy mouth he alwayes feeds
vpon the Syndrownd ſoule,
Whoſe gredy Pawes, do neuer ceas,
in ſynfull fluds to prowle.
Loe. This the ende, of euery ſuche
as here lyues luſtylye
Neglectyng God thou ſeeſt, in vyce.
do lyue. in ſyn do dye.
What ſhuld I ſpeke of al theyr harms
that happens them in lyfe ?
Theyr Conſcience prickt, theyr barren blud
theyr toyle, their grief, theyr ſtryfe,
With miſchiefes heaped many a one,
which they do neuer trye.
That Loue and Feare the myghty God,
that rules and raynes on hye,
To long it weare, to make diſcourſe,
and *Phebus* downe deſcends,
And in the Clowdes his beams doth hyde
which tempeſt ſure portends,
Looke how the beaſtes begin to fling,
and caſt theys heades on hye,
The Hearonſhew mountes aboue the clouds
ye Crowes ech wher do cry
All this ſhowes rayn, tyme byds vs go
com *Coridon* awaye,
Take vp thy Staffe, fetch in thy beaſts
let vs go whyle we maye.

Coridon. *Cornix* agreed, go thou before,
yon curſed Bull of myne
I muſt go dryue : he neuer bydes,
among my Fathers Kyne.

Finis Eglogæ octauæ.

EPYTAPHES.

¶ *An Epytaphe of the Lorde* Sheffeldes *death.*

WHen Brutyſh broyle, and rage of war
in Clownyſh harts began
When Tigres ſtoute, in Tanners bonde
vnmuſled all they ran,
The Noble Sheffeyld Lord by byrth
and of a courage good,
By clubbiſh hands, of crabbed Clowns
there ſpent his Noble blud.
His noble byrth auayled not,
his honor all was vayne,
Amyd the preaſe, of Maſtye Curres,
the valyant Lorde was ſlayne.
And after ſuche a ſorte (O ruth,)
that who can teares ſuppreſſe.
To thynke yat Dunghyll Dogs ſhuld dawnt
the Floure of worthynes.
Whyle as the rauenyng Wolues he prayed
his gylteles lyfe to ſaue.
A bluddy Butcher byg and blunt,
a vyle vnweldy knaue
With beaſtly blow of boyſterous byll
at hym (O Lorde) let dryue,
And clefte his head, and ſayd therwith
ſhalt thou be lefte alyue?
O Lorde that I had preſent ben,
and Hectors force withall,
Before that from his Carlyſh hands,
the cruell Byll dyd fall.
Then ſhulde that peaſaunt vyle haue felt
the clap vpon his Crowne,
Then ſhuld haue dazed his dogged hart
from dryuyng Lordes adowne.

Then ſhuld my hands haue ſaued thy lyfe
  good Lord whom deare I loued
Then ſhuld my hart in doutfull caſe,
  full well to the ben proued,
But all in vayne thy death I wayle,
  thy Corps in earth doth lye.
Thy kyng and Countrey for to ſerue
  thou dydſte not feare to dye.
Farewel good Lord, thy deth bewayle
  all ſuche as well the knewe,
And euerye man laments thy caſe:
  and *Googe* thy death doth rewe.

¶ *An Epytaphe of M.* Shelley *ſlayne at Muſſelbroughe.*

VVan Mars had moued mortall hate
  and forced fumyſh heate
And hye *Bellona* had decreed,
  to ſyt with Sworde in Seate,
The Scottes vntrue with ſyghtynge hande,
  theyr promys to denye,
Aſſembled faſt, and England thought,
  the trothe with them to trye.
Choſe *Muſcelbroughe* theyr ſyghtynge place
  amyd thoſe barrayne ſyelds
Theyr breche of ſayth, there not to try
  with trothe, but trotheles Shyeldes
In battayle braue, and Armye ſtrong
  Encamped ſure they laye,
Ten Scottes to one (a dredeful thyng
  a dolfull ſyghtyng daye.)
That Englyſh men were all agaſte,
  with quakyng ſtaues in hande.
To ſe theyr enemyes lye ſo neare,
  and death with them to ſtande.

No other remedye there was,
  but ſyght it out or flye.
And who ſhuld fyrſt the Onſet gyue,
  was ſure therin to dye.
Thus al diſmayde, and wrapt in feare
  with doutfull mynde they ſtande,
If beſt it be, with flyght of foote,
  to ſtryue or ſyght of hande.
Tyll at the length, a Captayn ſtoute.
  with hawtye mynde gan ſpeake.
O Cowards all, and maydly men
  of Courage faynt and weake,
Vnworthye com of Brutus race,
  to this your manhode gon,
And is there none you Daſtardes all,
  that dare them ſet vpon.
Then Shelly all inflamed with heate
  with heate of valyaunt mynde,
No Cowardes we, nor maydly men,
  ne yet of Daſtards kynde,
I wold you wyſte dyd euer com,
  but dare be bolde to trye,
Our manhode heare, thoughe nought appeare
  but deth to all mens eye
And with theſe wordes (O noble hart)
  no longer there he ſtayde,
But forth before them all he ſprang
  as one no whyt diſmayed
With charged ſtaffe on ſomyng horſe
  his Spurres with heeles he ſtrykes,
And forewarde ronnes with ſwiftye race,
  among the mortall Pykes
And in this race with famous ende,
  to do his Countrey good,
Gaue Onſet fyrſt vpon his Foes,
  and loſt his vitall blud.

¶ *Finis.*

ℂ *An Epytaphe of Maiſter* Thomas Phayre.

THe hawtye verſe, yat *Maro* wrote
made Rome to wonder muche
And meruayle none for why the Style
and waightynes was ſuche,
That all men iudged *Parnaſſus* Mownt
had clefte her ſelfe in twayne.
And brought forth one, that ſeemd to drop
from out *Mineruaes* brayne.
But wonder more, maye Bryttayne great
wher *Phayre* dyd floryſh late,
And barreyne tong with ſwete accord
reduced to ſuche eſtate :
That *Virgils* verſe hath greater grace
in forrayne foote obtaynde,
Than in his own, who whilſt he lyued
eche other Poets ſtaynde.
The Noble H. *Hawarde* once,
that raught eternall fame,
With mighty Style, did bryng a pece
Of *Virgils* worke in frame,
And *Grimaold* gaue the lyke attempt,
and *Douglas* wan the Ball,
whoſe famouſe wyt in Scottyſh ryme
had made an ende of all.
But all theſe ſame did *Phayre* excell,
I dare preſume to wryte,
As muche as doth *Appolloes* Beames.
the dymmeſt Starre in lyght.
The enuyous fates (O pytie great,
had great diſdayne to ſe,
That vs amongſt there ſhuld remayn
ſo fyne a wyt as he,

And in the mydſt oi all his toyle,
  dyd force hym hence to wende,
And leaue a Worke vnperſyt ſo,
  that neuer man ſhall ende.

¶ *An Epytaphe of the Death of* Nicolas Grimaold.

BEholde this fle=
tyng world how al things fade
  Howe euery thyng
doth paſſe and weare awaye,
Eche ſtate of lyfe,
by comon courſe and trade,
Abydes no tyme,
but hath a paſſyng daye.
For looke as lyfe,
that pleaſaunt Dame hath brought,
The pleaſaunt yeares,
and dayes of luſtynes,
So Death our Foe,
conſumeth all to nought,
Enuyeng theſe,
with Darte doth vs oppreſſe,
And that whiche is,
the greateſt gryfe of all,
The gredye Grype,
doth no eſtate reſpect,
But wher he comes,
he makes them down to fall,
Ne ſtayes he at,
the hie ſharpe wytted ſect.
For if that wytt,
or worthy Eloquens,
Or learnyng deape,
coulde moue hym to forbeare,

O *Grimaold* then,
thou hadſte not yet gon hence
But heare hadeſt ſene,
full many an aged yeare.
Ne had the Mu=
ſes loſte ſo fyne a Floure,
Nor had *Miner=*
ua wept to leaue the ſo,
If wyſdome myght
haue fled the fatall howre,
Thou hadſte not yet
ben ſuffred for to go,
A thouſande doltyſh
Geeſe we myght haue ſparde,
A thouſande wytles
heads, death might haue found
And taken them,
for whom no man had carde,
And layde them lowe,
in deepe obliuious grounde,
But Fortune fa=
ours Fooles as old men ſaye
And lets them lyue,
and take the wyſe awaye.

¶ *Finis.*

Sonettes.

¶ *To Mayster* Alexander Nowell.

THe Muses ioye,
and well they may to se,
So well theyr la=
boure com to good successe,
That they sustay=
ned long agoe in the,
Minerua smyles,
Phebus can do no lesse,
But ouer all,
they chyefly do reioyse,
That leauyng thyngs,
which are but fond and vayne,
Thou dyddest chuse,
(O good and happy choyse)
In sacred Scoles,
thy luckye yeares to trayne,
By whiche thou hast
obtaynde (O happy thyng)
To learne to lyue,
whyle other wander wyde,
And by thy lyfe,
to please the immortall kyng,
Then whiche so good,
nothyng can be applyed,
Lawe gyues the gayne,
and Physycke fyls the Purse,
Promotions hye,
gyues Artes to many one,
But this is it,
by whiche we scape the Curse,

And haue the blys
of God, when we be gone.
Is this but one=
ly Scriptures for to reade?
No, no. Not talke,
but lyfe gyues this in deade.

¶ *To Doctor* Bale.

GOod aged *Bale:*
that with thy hoary heares
Doſte yet perſyſte,
to turne the paynefull Booke,
O happye man,
that haſt obtaynde ſuche yeares,
And leavſt not yet,
on Papers pale to looke,
Gyue ouer now
to beate thy weryed brayne,
And reſt thy Pen
that long hath laboured ſoore
For aged men
vnſyt ſure is ſuche paine,
And the beſeems
to laboure now no more,
But thou I thynke
Don Platoes part will playe
With Booke in hand,
to haue thy dyeng daye.

¶ *Finis.*

¶ *To M.* Edwarde Cobham.

OLde *Socrates*,
whose wysdome dyd excell,
And past the reache,
of wysest in his tyme,
Surmounted all,
that on the earth dyd dwell,
That Craggye Hyls,
of vertue hye dyd clyme,
That *Socrates*,
my *Cobham* dyde allowe,
Eche man in youth,
hym selfe in Glasse to vew,
And wyld them oft,
to vse the same, but how ?
Not to delyght,
in forme of fadyng hew.
Nor to be proude
therof, as many be,
But for to stryue,
by beautie of the mynde,
For to adourne,
the beautie he doth se.
If warlyke forme,
Dame Nature hym assygnde,
By vertuous lyfe,
than countenaunce for to get,
That shall deface,
the fayrest of them all,
Suche Beautie as
no age nor yeares wyll fret :
That flyes with fame,
whan fyckle forme doth fayle,
Thus muche I saye,
that here to the present,

My wordes a Glaſſe
for the to looke vpon.
To the whom God,
in tender yeares hath lent,
A towardenes,
that maye be muſed vpon,
Suche towardenes,
as in more grauer yeares,
Doth ſure a hope,
of greater thyngs pretende,
Thy noble mynde,
that to thy frendes appeare,
Doth ſhowe the blud,
wherof thou doſte deſcende,
The gentlenes,
thou vſeſt vnto all ſuche,
As ſmallye haue
deſerued good wyll of the,
Doth ſhowe the grace,
thou haſt that ſure is muche,
As euer yet,
in any I dyd ſe,
That wyt as rype,
as Nature well can gyue,
Declares a grea=
ter hope than all the reſt,
That ſhall remayne,
to the whilſt thou doſte lyue,
In deſperate yls,
a Medycyne euer preſt.
Thy good behauyour,
of thy ſelfe in place
Wherſoeuer that
thou chaunceſt for to lyght,
So much both beautie,
mynde and wyt doth grace
As well can be
requyred of any wyght.

What ſteth now?
but onely God to prayſe,
Of whom thou haſt
receaued theſe Gyftes of thyne,
So ſhalt thou long,
lyue heare with happye dayes,
And after Death,
the ſtarrye Skyes ſhall clyme,
Let noughtye men,
ſaye what they lyſt to the,
Trade thou thy ſelfe,
in ſeruyng hym aboue,
No ſweter ſer=
uyce can deuyſed be,
Whom yf thou fearſt,
and faythfully doſte loue,
Be ſure no thyng,
on earth ſhall the annoye,
Be ſure he wyll,
the from eche harme defende,
Be ſure thou ſhalt,
long tyme thy lyfe enioye,
And after ma=
ny yeares to haue a bleſſed ende.

¶ *Finis.*

¶ *Of* Edwardes *of the Chappell.*

DEuyne *Camenes*
that with your ſacred food,
Haue fed and fo=
ſterde vp from tender yeares,
A happye man,
that in your fauour ſtoode
Edwards in Courte
that can not ſynde his feares

Your names be bleſt,
that in this preſent age
So fyne a head,
by Arte haue framed out
Whom ſome hereaf=
ter helpt by Poets rage,
Perchaunce maye matche,
but none ſhall paſſe (no doubt)
O *Plautus* yf
thou wert alyue agayne,
That Comedies
ſo fynely dydſte endyte.
Or *Terence* thou
that with thy pleſaunt brayne,
The hearers mynde
on ſtage dydſt much delyght.
What wold you ſay
ſyrs if you ſhould beholde,
As I haue done
the doyngs of this man?
No word at all
to ſweare I durſt be bolde,
But burne with teares,
that which with myrth began,
I meane your bookes,
by which you gate your name,
To be forgot,
you wolde commit to flame.
Alas I wolde
Edvvards more tell thy prayſe,
But at thy name
my muſe amaſed ſtayes.

To L. Blundeſton.

SOme men be coun=
tyd wyſe that well can talke :
And ſome becauſe

they can eche man begyle.
Some forbecaufe
they know well chefe from chalke,
And can be fure,
weepe who fo lyft to fmyle.
But (Blundfton) hym
I call the wyfeft wyght,
Whom God gyues grace
to rule affections ryght.

The Aunfwere of L. Blundefton *to the fame.*

AFfections feekes
hygh honours frayle eftate,
Affections doth
the golden meane reproue.
Affections tourns
the frendly hart to hate,
Affections breedes
without difcretion Loue,
Both wyfe and
happye (*Googe*) he maye be hyght,
Whom God gyues grace,
to rule affections ryght.

❡ *To* Alexander Neuell.

THe lytell Fyfh,
that in the ftreme doth fleet
With brode forth ftret-
ched Fyns for his difporte
When as he fpyes,
the Fyffhes bayte fo fwete,
In hafte he hyes,
fearynge to com to fhorte,

But all to ſoone
(alas) his gredy mynde,
By raſh attempt,
doth bryng hym to his bane,
for where he thought
a great relyeſe to fynde,
By hydden hooke,
the ſymple fole is tane.
So fareth man,
that wanders here and theare,
Thynkyng no hurt
to happen hym therbye,
He ronnes amayne,
to gaſe on Beauties cheare,
Takes all for golde
that glyſters in the eye,
And neuer leaues
to feade by lookyng long,
On Beauties Bayte,
where Bondage lyes enwrapt,
Bondage that makes
hym to ſynge an other ſong,
And makes hym curſe
the bayte that hym entrapte.
Neuell to the,
that loueſt their wanton lookes,
Feade on the bayte,
but yet beware the Hookes.

Alexander Neuells *Anſwere to the ſame.*

IT is not curſed *Cupids* Dart :
Nor *Venus* cancred Spyght,
It is not vengeaunce of the Gods
That wretched harts doth ſmyght,
With reſtleſſe rage of carefull Loue.
No, No, thy Force alone

Affection ſond, doth ſtyr theſe flames.
 Thou cauſeſt vs to mone
And waile, and curs our wretched ſtats.
 Our thryſe vnhappy plights,
Our ſighes, and powdred ſobs with tears,
 Our greuous gronyng Sprights,
Thy hateful Malice doth procure:
 O Fancye flamyng Feend
Of Hel. For thou in outwarde ſhape,
 And colour of a frende
Doſt by thy Snares and ſlymed Hooks
 entrap the wounded Harts:
From whence theſe Hellike torments ſpryng,
 and euer greauyng Smarts.
Whence Gripe of minde, with chaunged chere
 Whence face beſmeard with teares.
Whence thouſand miſchiefs more, wherwith
 ſuche Myſers liues outweares.
Our gaſyng eyes on Bewties bayt
 do worke our endles bane.
Our eyes I ſay doo worke our woo,
 Our eyes procure our paine.
Theie are the Traps to vexed mynds
 Here Gyns and Snares do lye.
Here ſyre and flames by Fancie framde,
 In breſt doo broyle and frye.
O *Googe* the Bayte ſone ſpyed is.
 Soone vewd their wanton lookes.
Wheron to feede, and yet to ſhun,
 The priuy lurkyng hookes,
Their pain, Their toile, Their labour is
 There There lyes endles ſtriſe.
O happy than that Man account,
 Whoſe well directed Lyte
Can fly thoſe yls, which ſancy ſtirs,
 And lyue from Bondage free.
A *Phœnix* ryght on yearth (no doubte)
 A Byrde full rare to ſee.

¶ *To M.* Henrye Cobham, *of the moſt bleſſed ſtate of Lyfe.*

THe happyeſt lyfe
that here we haue,
My *Cobham* yf
I ſhall defyne,
The goodlyeſt ſtate,
twyxte byrth and graue.
Moſt gracious
dayes and ſweteſt tyme,
The fayreſt face,
of fadynge Lyfe,
Race ryghtlyeſt ronne
in ruthfull wayes,
The ſafeſt meanes
to ſhun all ſtryfe:
The ſureſt Staffe,
in fyckle Dayes:
I take not I
as ſome do take,
To gape and gawne,
for Honours hye,
But Court and
Cayſer to forſake,
And lyue at home,
full quyetlye,
Remembreſt thou?
what he once ſayde,
Who bad, Courte not
in any caſe,
For Vertue is,
in Courtes decayed,
And Vyce with States,
hath chyefeſt place,

Not Courte but Countreye
I do iudge,
Is it wheare lyes,
the happyeſt lyfe,
In Countreye growes,
no gratynge grudge,
In Countreye ſtandes
not ſturdye ſtryſe,
In Countreye,
Bacchus hath no place,
In Countreye
Venus hath defecte,
In Countreye
Thraſo hath no grace,
In Countreye
ſewe of *Gnatoes* Secte.
But theſe ſame foure
and many more,
In Courte,
thou ſhalt be ſure to fynde,
For they haue vowed,
not thence to goe,
Bycauſe in Courte,
dwels ydle mynde.
In Countreye
mayſte thou ſafelye reſt,
And flye all theſe,
yf that thou lyſte,
The Countrey therfore,
iudge I beſt,
Where godly lyfe,
doth vyce reſyſte,
Where vertuous
exercyſe with ioye,
Doth ſpende the yeares
that are to run,
Where Vyces fewe,
maye the annoye,
This lyfe is beſt
whan all is done.

¶ *To* Alexander Neuell *of the blessed State of him that feeles not the force of Cupids flames.*

AS ofte as I
remembre with my self,
The Fancies fonde,
that flame by foolysh Loue,
And marke the Furyes
fell, the blynded elfe
And Venus she
that raynes so sore aboue,
As ofte as I
do se the wofull state,
Of Louers all,
and eake their myserye,
The ones desy=
ryng mynde the others hate,
Trothe with the one,
with the other Trecherye,
So ofte say I,
that blessed in the wyght,
Yea *Neuell* blest,
and double blest agayne,
That can by rea=
son rule hys mynde a ryght,
And take suche foo-
lysh fadynge toyes for vayne.

¶ Alexander Neuells *Awnswere to the same.*

THe plunged mind in fluds of griefs
The Sences drowned quyght,
The Hart opprest. The flesh consumed
The chaunged state outright.

The Body dryed by broylyng blafe,
Of preuy fchorchyng Flame.
The doulfull Face. The countnaunce fad
The drowping Courage tame.
The Scaldyng fyghes. The greeuous groones
The burning rage of fyre
The erneft fute. The fruitles Toyle.
The deepe and hot Defyre,
The Braynes quight brufd and crufht with Cares.
The euer duryng foore.
The very paynes of Hell it felf,
with thoufande mifchyefes moore,
Which wounded Harts enflamed with Loue
with Gryefe do ouerflow,
And works theyr endles plage and fpight
Tyll Death from thence do growe.
All thefe conclude him bleft (my *Googe*)
And trible bleft agayne,
That taught bi tract of Time can take
Such fadyng Toyes for vayne.

¶ *To Mayftreffe* A.

SYnce I fo long haue lyved in pain
and burnt for loue of the,
(O cruel hart) dofte thou no more
efteame the Loue of me,
Regardft thou not, the health of hym?
that the, aboue the reft
Of Creatures all, and next to God
hath deareft in his breft.
Is pytie placed from the fo farre
is gentlenes exylde?
Haft thou ben foftred in the Caues,
of Wolues or Lyons wylde?
Haft thou ben fo? why then no force,
the leffe I meruayle I,
Such as the Damme, fuche is the yong
experyence trewe doth trye.

Syth thou art of ſo fyerce a mynde,
  why dyd not God then place
In the, with ſuche a Tygers Harte,
  a ſowle yll ſauerde face?
Sure for no other ende but that,
  he lykes no Louers trade,
And the therfore a ragynge Fende,
  an Angels face hath made.
Suche one as thou, was *Gorgon* ones
  as auncient Poets tell,
Who with her Beautie mazed men,
  and nowe doth raygne in Hell,
But mercye yet, of the I craue,
  yf ought in the remayne,
And let me not ſo long the force,
  of flamyng fyre ſuſtayne,
Let pytie ioynde with beautie be,
  ſo ſhall I not dyſdayne,
My blud, my hart, my lyfe to ſpende
  with toyle, with ſtryſe, and payne,
To do the good, my breath to looſe,
  yf nede ſhall ſo requyre,
But for my ſeruyce and my paynes,
  thou gyueſt me hate for hyre.
Well now take this for ende of all,
  I loue and thou doſte hate,
Thou lyueſt in pleaſures happely.
  and I in wretched ſtate.
Paynes can not laſt for euermore,
  but tyme and ende wyll trye,
And tyme ſhall tell me in my age,
  How youth led me awrye.
Thy face that me tormented, ſo,
  in tyme ſhall ſure decaye,
And all that I do lyke or loue,
  ſhall vanyſh quyte awaye,
Thy face in tyme ſhall wrynckled be,
  at whiche I ſhall be glad,

To ſee thy forme transformed thus,
that made me once ſo ſad,
Than ſhall I blame my foly moch
and thanke the mightyeſt kyng
That hath me ſaued tyll ſuch a daye,
to ſe ſo fonde a thyng.
And tyll that tyme I wyll keepe cloſe
my flames and let them blaſe,
All ſecretly within my breſt,
no man on me ſhall gaſe.
I wyll not treſpaſſe ſynfully,
for God ſhall geue me grace
To ſe the tyme wherin I ſhall
neglecte thy folyſh face,
And tyll that tyme adieu to thee,
God keepe thee far from me,
And ſende thee in that place to dwell,
that I ſhall neuer ſee.

¶ *To* George Holmeden *of a ronnynge Heade.*

THe greateſt vyce
that happens vnto men,
And yet a vyce,
that many comon haue,
As auncient Wryters
waye with ſobre Pen,
Who gaue theyr doome,
by force of wyſdom graue,
The foreſt mayme,
the greateſt euyll ſure,
The vyleſt plague
that Students can ſuſtayne,
And that whiche moſte
doth ygnoraunce procure.
My *Holmeden* is
to haue a ronnynge Brayne,

For who is he
that leades more reſtles lyfe,
Or who can euer
lyue more yll beſtead?
In fyne who lyues,
in greater Care and ſtryfe,
Then he that hath,
ſuche an vnſtedfaſt hedde:
But what is this?
me thynkes I heare the ſay,
Phyſition take,
thine owne diſeaſe away.

¶ *To the Tranſlation of Pallingen.*

THe labour ſwete,
that I ſuſtaynde in the,
(O *Pallingen*)
when I tooke Pen in hande,
Doth greue me now,
as ofte as I the ſe,
But halfe hewd out
before myne eyes to ſtande,
For I muſt needes
(no helpe) a whyle go toyle,
In Studyes, that
no kynde of muſe delyght.
And put my Plow,
in groſſe vntylled ſoyle,
And labour thus,
with ouer weryed Spryght,
But yf that God,
do graunt me greater yeares.
And take me not
from hence, before my tyme,
The Muſes nyne,
the pleaſaunt ſynging feares

Shall ſo enflame
my mynde with luſt to ryme,
That *Palingen*
I wyll not leaue the ſo,
But ſynyſh the
accordyng to my mynd.
And yf it be
my chaunce away to go,
Let ſome the ende,
that heare remayne behynde.

¶ *The Harte abſent.*

SWete muſe tell me,
wher is my hart becom,
For well I feele,
it is from hence a way,
My Sences all,
doth ſorrow ſo benumme:
That abſent thus,
I can not lyue a Day.
I know for troth,
there is a ſpecyall Place,
Wher as it moſt,
deſyreth for to bee:
For Oft it leaues,
me thus in Dolſull caſe,
And hether commes,
at length a gayne to me?
Woldeſt thou ſo fayne,
be tolde where is thy Harte
Sir Foole in place,
wher as it ſhuld not be:
Tyed vp ſo faſt,
that it can neuer ſtarte?
Tyll Wyſdom get,
agayne thy Lybertye:
In place wher thou,

as ſafe maiſt dwel ſwet daw?
As may the harte,
ly by the Lyons paw:
And wher for thee,
as much be ſure they paſſe:
As dyd the maſter
ons for *Eſops* Aſſe.

¶ *To* Alexander Neuell.

IF thou canſt baniſh Idle nes,
  Cupidoes Bowe is broke, *Ouid.*
And well thou mayſt dyſpyſe his bronds
  cleane void of flame and ſmoke
What moued the Kynge *Agiſtus* ons,
  to Loue with vyle exceſſe:
The cauſe at hand doth ſtreight apeare
  he lyued in Idlenes.

Finis.

¶ *The Aunſwere of* A. Neuell *to the ſame.*

THe lack of labour mayms ye mind,
And wyt and Reaſon quyght exiles.
And Reaſon fled. Flames Fancy blind.
And Fancy ſhe forthwith beguyles
The Senſles wight: that ſwiftly ſails
Through deepeſt fluds of vyle exces.
Thus vice abounds. Thus vertu quails
By meanes of drowſy Idlenes.

¶ *To Mayſtreſſe* D.

NOt from the hye *Cytherion* Hyll
  nor from that Ladies throne
From whens flies forth ye winged boy

yat makes ſome ſore to grone.
But nearer hence this token coms,
from out the Dongeon deepe,
Where neuer Plutto yet dyd raygne
nor Proſerpyne dyd ſleepe.
Wheras thy faithful Seruaunt liues.
whom duetie moues aryght,
To wayle that he ſo long doth lacke,
his owne deare Mayſtres ſyght.

❡ *Out of an olde Poet.*

FYe Fye, I lothe
to ſpeake wylt thou my luſt,
Compell me nowe,
to doo ſo foule an acte.
Nay rather God
with Flame conſume to duſt.
My carryon vyle,
then I perfourme this facte
Let rather thoughtes,
that long, haue weryed me:
Or ſycknes ſuche
as Fancye fonde hath brought,
O gapyng Hell,
dryne me now downe to the,
Let boylyng ſyghes,
conſume me all to nought.

ONs muſynge as I ſat,
and Candle burnynge bye,
When all were huſht I myght diſcern
a ſymple ſelye Flye.
❡ That flewe before myne eyes,
with free reioyſynge Hart,
And here and there, with wings did play
as voyde of payne and ſmart,

¶ Somtyme by me ſhe ſat,
  when ſhe had playde her fyll,
And euer when ſhe reſted had
  aboute ſhe flyttered ſtyll.
¶ When I perceyued her well,
  reioyſyng in her place,
O happye Flye quoth I, and eake,
  O worme in happy caſe.
¶ Whiche two of vs is beſt?
  I that haue reaſon? no:
But thou that reaſon art without
  and therwith voyde of woe.
¶ I lyue and ſo doſte thou,
  but I lyue all in payne,
And Subiect am to her alas,
  that makes my Gryefe her gayne.

[The following lines are added to this Poem, in the *Faultes escaped, &c.* at the end of the original Edition.]

¶ Thou lyueſt, but feelſt no gryefe,
  no Loue doth the torment,
A happye thynge for me it were,
  If God were ſo content.
That thou with Pen, wert placed here
  and I ſat in thy place,
Then I ſhuld Ioye as thou doſt nowe
  and thau ſhuldſt wayle thy caſe.

WHen I do heare thy name,
  alas my hart doth ryſe:
And ſeekes fourthwith to ſe the ſalue
  that moſt contentes myne eys.
But when I ſe thy Face,
  that hath procured my payne,

Then boyles my blud in euery part,
  and beates in euery vayne?
Thy voice when I do heare,
  then collour comes and goes,
Some tyme as pale as Earth I looke,
  ſome tyme as red as Roſe.
If thy ſweete Face do ſmyle,
  then who ſo well as I?
If thou but caſt a ſcornefull looke,
  then out alas I dye.
But ſtyll I lyue in payne,
  my fortune wylleth ſo,
That I ſhuld burne and thou yet know,
  no whytt of all my wo.

VNhappye tonge
why dydſte thou not conſent
When fyrſt myne eyes
dyd vewe that Princely face,
To ſhow good wyll,
that hart oppreſt than ment.
And whylſt tyme was,
to ſewe for preſent grace.
O ſayntyng Hart,
why dydſt thou then conceale?
Thyne inwarde Fyers,
that flamde in euery vayne,
Whan pytie and
gentlenes, were bent to heale.
Why dydſt thou not,
declare thy ragyng payne?
When well thou mightſt
haue moued her gentle mynde,
Why dydſte thou than,
kepe backe thy wofull playn?

Thou knewſte full well,
redres is hard to ſynde,
Whan in thy owne
affayres, thy corage faynts.
But ſynce ſhe is
gon, bewaile thy grief no moore
Synce thou thy ſelfe,
wart Cauſer of the Soore.

ℭ *Oculi augent dolorem.*
Out of ſyght, out of mynd.

THe oftener ſene, the more I luſt,
The more I luſt, the more I ſmart
The more I ſmart, the more I truſt,
The more I truſt, the heauyer hart,
The heuy hart, breedes myne vnreſt,
Thy abſence therfore, lyke I beſt.

The rarer ſene, the leſſe in mynde,
The leſſe in mynde, the leſſer payne,
The leſſer payne, leſſe gryefe I ſynd,
The leſſer gryefe, the greater gayne,
The greater gayne, the meryer I,
Therfore I wyſh thy ſyght to flye.

The further of, the more I ioye.
The more I ioye, the happyer lyfe,
The happyer lyfe, leſſe hurts annoye
The leſſer hurts, pleaſure moſt ryſe,
Suche pleaſures ryſe, ſhall I obtayne
When Diſtaunce doth depart vs twaine.

ℭ *Finis.*

ACcuse not God, yf fancie fond,
do moue thy foolysh brayne,
To wayle for loue, for thou thy selse,
art cause of all thy payne.

☙ *Finis.*

TWo Lynes shall tell the Gryefe
that I by Loue sustayne.
I burne, I flame, I faynt, I fryse,
of Hell I feele the payne.

☙ *Of the vnfortunate choyse of his Valentyne.*

THe Paynes that all the Furyes fell
can cast from Lymbo lake,
Eche Torment of those Hellish brains
wher crawleth mani a snake,
Eche mischiefe that therin doth lye
eche smart that may be founde,
Flye from those feendish clawes a whyle
with flames breake vp the grounde,
Lyght here vpon this cursed hand,
make here your dwellyng place,
And plague the part, yat durst presume
his Mayster to disgrace.
Which thrust amonge a nombre of:
so many princely names,
And wher thy Maistres had her place
amongst the chiefest Dames,
Durste thus presume to leue her there
and drawe a straunger wyght,
And by thyne owne vnhappy draught
torment my pauled Spryght.

❡ *The vncertayntie of Lyfe.*

NO vayner thing ther can be found
  amyd this vale of ſtryfe,
As Auncient men reporte haue made
  then truſte vncertayne lyfe.
This tr[e]we we dayly fynde,
  by proofes of many yeares,
And many tymes the trothe is tryed,
  by loſſe of frendly fears,
Hope who ſo lyſt in lyfe
  hath but vncertayne ſtay.
As tayle of Ele that harder held,
  doth ſooner ſlyde away.
When leaſt we thynk therof,
  moſt neare approcheth it.
And ſodaynly poſſes the place,
  wher lyfe before did ſytt:
How many haue byn ſeen,
  in Helth to go to reſt,
And yet eare mornyng tyde haue ben,
  with Cruell Death oppreſt,
How many in their meales,
  Haue Ioyfully ben ſett,
That ſodaynly in all their Feaſte,
  hath yealded Earth theyr dett.
Syth thus the lyfe is nought,
  that in this world we truſt,
And that for all the pompe and Pryde,
  the Bodie tournes to duſt:
Hope for the lyfe a boue,
  whiche far ſurmounteth all.
With vertuous mind await the time
When God, for vs doth call.

¶ *A Refusall.*

SYth Fortune fauoures not
 and al thynges backward go,
And syth your mynd, hath so decreed,
 to make an end of woe.
Syth now is no redresse,
 but hence I must a way,
Farwele I wast no vayner wordes,
 I Hope for better day.

¶ *Of Maistres* D S.

THy fyled wordes,
yat from thy mouth did flow
Thy modest looke
with gesture of *Diane.*
Thy curteous mynde,
and althynges framed so.
As answered well,
vnto thy vertuous fame,
The gentlenes
that at thy handes I founde
In straungers hou[s]e,
all vnaquaynted I,
Good S. hath
my Hart to the so bounde,
That from the can
it not be forced to flye,
In pledge wherof,
my seruyce here I gyue
Yf thou so wylte
to serue the whylst I lyue.

¶ *Of Money.*

GYue Money me, take
Frendſhyp who ſo lyſt,
For Frends are gon
come once Aduerſytie,
When Money yet
remayneth ſafe in Cheſt,
That quickely can the
bryng from myſerye,
Fayre face ſhowe frendes,
whan ryches do haboundc,
Come tyme of proofe,
farewell they muſt awaye,
Beleue me well,
they are not to be founde.
If God but ſende
the once a lowrynge daye.
Golde neuer ſtarts
aſyde, but in dyſtres,
Fyndes wayes enoughe,
to eaſe thyne heuynes.

¶ *Goyng towardes Spayne.*

FArewell thou fertyll ſoyle,
that *Brutus* ſyrſt out founde,
When he poore ſoule, was driuen clean
from out his Countrey ground.
That Northward layſt thy luſty ſides
amyd the ragyng Seas.
Whoſe welthy Land doth foſter vpp,
thy people all in eaſe,
While others ſcrape and carke abroad,
theyr ſymple foode to gett.

And ſelye Soules toke all for good,
  that commeth to the Net.
Which they with painfull paynes do py[n]ch.
  in barrain burning Realmes:
While we haue all with out reſtreint
  a mong thy welthy ſtreames.
O bleſt of God thou Pleaſaunt Ile,
  where welth her ſelf doth dwell:
Wherin my tender yeares I paſt
  I byd thee now farewell.
For Fancy dryues me forth abrode,
  and byds me take delyght,
In leuyng thee and raungyng far,
  to ſee ſome ſtraunger ſyght.
And ſayth I was not framed heare
  to lyue at home with eas:
But paſſynge forth for knowledge ſake
  to cut the ſomyng ſeas.

❡ *At Bonyuall in Fraunce.*

O Fond affectyon
wounder of my Hart,
When wylt thou Ceaſe,
to breed my reſtles payne,
When comes the end,
of this my Cruell ſmart:
When ſhall my force,
beate backe thy force agayne.
When ſhall I ſaye,
this reſtles rage of myne:
By Reaſon ruld,
is banyſht quyght a way,
And I eſcaped,
theſe cruell bondes of thyne:
O flamynge feend,
that ſeakeſt my decaye.

Safe thynkyng I,
Charibdis Rage to flye,
On Scylla Rocke,
in Bonyuall I dye.

ℭ *Commynge home warde out of Spayne.*

O Ragyng Seas,
and myghty Neptunes rayne,
In monſtrous Hylles,
that throweſt thy ſelfe ſo hye,
That wyth thy fludes,
doeſt beate the ſhores of Spayne:
And breake the Clyues,
that dare thy force enuie.
Ceaſe now thy rage,
and laye thyne Ire a ſyde,
And thou that haſt,
the gouernaunce of all,
O myghty God,
grant Wether Wynd and Tyde,
Tyll on my Coun-
treye Coaſt, our Anker fall.

ℭ *To* L. Blundeſton *of Ingratitude.*

THe lytell Byrde,
the tender Marlyon,
That vſeth ofte
vpon the Larke to praye,
With great reproche,
doth ſtayne the mynde of man
If all be true,
that Wryters of her ſaye.
For ſhe a Creature,
maymde of Reaſons parte,
And framde to lyue
accordynge to her kynde,

Doth ſeme to foſter
Reaſon in her Hart
And to aſpyre
vnto Deuyner mynde.
when Hungers rage
ſhe hath exyled quyte,
And ſupped well
as falleth for her ſtate.
The ſelye Larke,
doth take by force of flyght,
And hyes to tree,
where as ſhe lodged late,
And on the trem-
blyng Byrde all nyght ſhe ſtondes,
To keepe her feete,
from force of nyppynge colde,
The amazed Wretche,
within her ennemyes handes,
And cloſed faſt,
within the claſpyng holde.
Awayteth Death,
with drowſye drowpyng Hart,
And all the nyght
with feare drawes on her lyfe,
The gentle Byrde,
whan darkenes doth departe
Doth not depryue,
the ſelye ſoule of lyfe,
Nor fylles with her
her hungred egre breſt
But wayeng well,
the ſeruyce ſhe hath done.
To ſpyll the Blud,
her Nature doth deteſt,
And from ſo great
a Cryme, her ſelfe doth ſhun.
She lets her go
and more with ſtedfaſt eyes.
Beholds whiche way

ſhe takes with mazed flight,
And in thoſe partes
that Daye ſhe neuer flyes
Leaſt on that Byrde
agayne ſhe chaunce to lyght.
Loe, *Blundſton* heare
how kyndenes doth haboundc,
In ſelye Soules
where Reaſon is exylde,
This Byrde alone
ſuffyſeth to confounde,
The Brutyſh myndes
of men that are defyled,
With that great Vice,
that vyle and haynous Cryme
Ingratitude
(whiche ſome vnkyndenes call.)
That Poyſon ſtrong
that ſpryngeth ſtyll with tyme,
Tyll at the length,
it hath infected all.

☾ *The Aunſwere of* L. Blundeſton *to the ſame.*

THis Mirrour left
of this thy Byrde I fynde,
Hath not ſuche force,
to enter in the Hert,
To roote away
Vnthankefulnes of minde,
As others haue,
the Vertues to peruert,
(ſo prone we are to Vice :)
The Tenche by kynd
hath Salue for euery Soore,
And heales the may-
med Pike in his dyſtreſſe,

The Churlyſh Pike
for gentlenes therfore,
In his rewarde,
doth cruellye expreſſe.
His murdring mynde,
his fylthy ſpotted fayth,
When hungre prickes
to fyll his gredye Iawes,
He grypes his poore
Chyrurgion vnto death.
Who late to hym
of lyfe was onely cauſe.
Thy Merlians haue
fewe Ayryes in our ground
But Pikes haue Spawnes
good ſtoore in euery Pound.

¶ *To the Tune of Appelles.*

THe ruſhyng Ryuers that do run
The valeys ſweet adourned new
That leans their ſides againſt ye Sun
with Flours freſh of ſundry hew,
Both Aſhe and Elme, and Oke ſo hye,
Do all lament my wofull crye.

while winter blak, with hydious ſtormes
Doth ſpoil ye ground of Sommers grene,
while ſpringtime ſweet ye leaf returns
That late on tree could not be ſene,
while ſomer burns while harueſt rains
Stil ſtyl do rage my reſtles paynes.

No ende I find in all my ſmart,
But endles torment I ſuſtayne
Synce fyrſt alas, my wofull Hart
By ſight of the was forſt to playne,
Synce that I loſt my Lybertie,
Synce that thou madſte a Slaue of me

My Hart that once abroade was free
Thy Beautie hath in durance brought
Ons reaſon rulde and guyded me,
And how is wyt conſumde with thought
Ons I reioyſed aboue the Skye,
And now for the I alas I dye.

Ons I reioyſed in Companye,
And now my chief and whole delyght
Is from my frendes awaye to flye
And keepe alone my weryed ſpryght
Thy face deuyne and my deſyre,
From fleſh hath me tranſformed to fyre.

O Nature thou that fyrſt dyd frame,
My Ladyes heare of pureſt Golde
Her face of Cryſtall to the ſame.
Her lippes of precious Rubyes molde
Her necke of Alablaſter whyte
Surmountyng far eche other Wight

Why dydſt thou not that tyme deuiſe
Why dydſt thou not foreſe before?
The miſchyefe that therof doth ryſe,
And grief on grief doth heap with ſtor
To make her Hart of Wax alone,
And not of Flynt and Marble Stone.

O Lady ſhowe thy fauour yet,
Let not thy Seruaunt dye for the
Where Rygour rulde, let Mercy ſyt
Let Pytie Conquere Crueltie
Let not Diſdain, a Feend of Hell,
Poſſes the place, wher Grace ſhould dwell.

❡ Cupido Conquered.

THe ſweeteſt time of al the yeare
it was when as the Sonne,
Had newly entred *Gemini*,
and warmynge heate begun:
Whan euery tre was clothed greene,
and flowers fayre dyd ſhow,
And when the whyt and blowmynge
on Hawthorns thicke did grow,
Whan ſore I longd to ſeeke a broade,
to ſe ſome Pleaſaunt ſyght,
A mid my woes and heauye happes,
that myght my Mynde delyght,
Care wold not let me byde within
but forſt me foorth to go:
And bad me ſeeke ſume preſent helpe,
for to relyue my wo.
Than forward went I foorth in haſte,
to vew the garnyſht trees?
What tyme the Son was mounted vp,
twixt nyne and ten degrees.
From Flowers flew ſweete ayers abroad,
delighting much my brayn,
With ſyght and ſmels gan ſorow fade,
and Ioy returne agayne.
So that in mynde I much reioyce,
to feele my ſelf ſo lyght:
For gorgyous ſyghtes and odours ſweet
had new reuyued my ſpryght.
Beſyde the pleaſaunt Harmonye,
that ſyngyng Byrdes did make:
Bad me pul vpp my Hart agayne,
and ſorrow ſone forſake.
For though (quoth *Reaſon.*) ſhe be gon
on whom thy Lyfe dependes,

Yet fond it is to carke and care
 where there is none amendes.
Thus foorth I went, and in the grooues
 I raunged heare and theare,
Wheras I hard ſuche pleaſaunt tunes
 as Heauen had ben neare.
I thynke that if *Amphion* hadde,
 ben preſent ther to playe,
Or if Sir *Orpheus* myght haue held,
 his Harp, that preſent day.
Or if *Apollo* with his Lute,
 had ſtryuen to excell,
None of them all, by Muſycke ſholde,
 haue borne away the Bell.
I rather iudge the thracian wold,
 his Harpe wherwith he played,
Haue caſt a way as one whom Ire,
 had vtterly diſmayed.
Such paſſyng tunes of ſundry Byrds,
 I neuer herd before,
The further I went in the Woods.
 the noyſe reſounded more.
O happy Byrdes quoth I what lyfe,
 is this that you do leade,
How far from Care and myſery,
 how far from Feare and dread:
With what reioyſynge melodie,
 paſſe you this ſadyng Lyfe,
While Man vnhappieſt creatur liues
 In wretched toyle and ſtryſe.
Styll foorth I went and wonderd at,
 this pleſaunt Harmony.
And gaſed at theſe lytle Fooles,
 that made ſuche Melody:
Tyll at the length I gan to ſpye,
 a ſtately Lawrell tree,
So plaſt and ſett in ſuch a guyſe,
 That as it ſeamed to me,

Dame Nature ſtroue to ſhew her ſelf
  in plantyng ſuch a thyng,
For Euen out beſyde the rocke,
  a ſountayne cleane did ſpryng,
Where in the water I beheld,
  reſembled wonderous trew,
The Whyte and Greene of al the trees,
  adourned late of new.
And how in order eake they ſtood,
  a goodly ſyght to ſe,
And there I might diſcerne the Byrds
  that ſonge in euery tree.
To moue the Byll and ſhake the wings
  in vteryng Muſicke ſweete
And heare and thear, to flye to ſeade,
  and eſteſones theare to meete.
Great pleaſure had I there to byde,
  and ſtare vpon the Spryng,
For why me thought it dyd ſurmount,
  eache other kynde of thyng.
Now was the Son got vp aloſt,
  and raught the mydle Lyne,
And in the Well, the Golden Gloobe,
  with flamyng Beames dyd ſhyne,
Wherof the Bryghtnes was ſo great.
  that I might not endure,
Lenger to looke within the Spryng,
  whoſe waters were ſo pure.
Vnwyllyng went I thence away,
  and vnderneth the tree,
I laid me down whoſe braunches brode
  dyd keepe the Son from me.
Thynkyng to reſt me there a whyle,
  tyll ſallyng ſome degrees
Syr Phebus ſhuld haue hyd hym ſelf,
  behynde the ſhadowyng trees,
And then for to haue vewd the Spring,
  and marked euery place,

And ſeene yf there I could haue ſpied
  the weepyng *Biblis* face.
For ſure I thynke, it was the place,
  wherein *Narciſſus* dyed,
Or els the Well, to which was turnd
  poore *Biblis* whyle ſhe cryed.
But whether it was werynes,
  with labour that I tooke,
Or Fume yat from the Spryng dyd ryſe,
  wherin I late dyd looke.
Or yf it were the ſweete accorde
  that ſyngyng Byrdes dyd keepe,
Or what it was, I knowe no whit
  but I fell faſt a ſleepe.
I thynke the woddy Nimphes agreed
  that I ſhuld haue this chaunce,
And that it was theyr pleaſure ſo,
  to ſhowe me thyngs in traunce.
Whilſte I lay thus in ſlumbre deepe,
  I myght perceyue to ſtande,
A Perſon clothed all in whyte,
  that held a Rod in hande.
Whiche was me thought of Maſſey Golde.
  I knew it very weale,
For that was it, made *Argos* ſleepe,
  whyle he dyd *Io* ſteale.
When I perceaued by his attyre,
  that it was *Mercuri.*
My Hart at fyrſt began to faynt,
  yet at the length quoth I
Thou Goddeſſe Son, why ſtandſte you there
  what buſines now with thee,
What meaneſt you in thy flying weed,
  For to appeare to me,
And therwithall my thought I ſtaied,
  and could no farther ſpeake,
For Feare did force my ſpeech to fayle,
  and Courage waxed weake.

Which whan the ſone of *Maia* ſawe,
he tooke me by the hand,
Looke vp quoth he be not affrayed:
but boldly by me ſtand.
The Muſes all of *Helicon*,
haue ſent me now to thee:
Whom thou doeſt ſerue and whoſe you ſekſt
For euer more to be.
And thankes to the by me they ſende,
Bycauſe thou tookeſt payne,
In theyr Affaires (a thankeles thyng)
to occupie thy Brayne.
Deſyring thee not for to ſtaye,
for *Momus* ill report,
But endyng that thou haſt begun,
to ſpyte the Canckred ſorte.
And thynk not thou, that thou art he,
that canſt eſcape Diſdayne,
The day ſhall come when thankfull men,
ſhall well accept thy Paine,
But rather lay before thyne eyes,
the hie attemptes of thoſe,
Whoſe ſtatly ſtyle with painfull proofe,
theyr worthy wytes diſcloſe,
Marke him that thundred out ye deeds
Of olde *Anchiſes* ſun,
Whoſe Engliſh verſe gyues *Maroes* grace,
In all that he hath done,
Whoſe death the *Muſes* ſorrow much,
that lacke of aged dayes,
Amongeſt the common Brytons old,
ſhould hynder *Virgils* prayſe.
Mark him yat hath wel framde a Glaſſe
for ſtates to looke vpon,
Whoſe labour ſhews the ends of them
that lyued long a gone.
Marke hym that ſhowes ye Tragedies
thyne owne famylyar Frende,

By whom ye Spaniards hawty Style
 in Englyſh Verſe is pende.
Marke theſe ſame three, and other moe,
 whoſe doyngs well are knowne,
Whoſe fayre attempts in euery place
 The flying ſame hath blowne,
Haſt thou not harde, thyſelf in place
 full ofte and many a tyme,
Lo here the Auctor loſeth grace,
 Loe here a doltyſh Ryme,
Now ſyth that they haue this reward
 who paſſe the euen as farre,
As in the nyght *Diana* doth,
 Excell the dimmeſt Starre.
Take thou no ſcorne at euyll tongs,
 what neadſt thou to diſdayne?
Syth they whom none can well amend
 haue lyke fruyte of theyr payne.
Moreouer yet the Ladyes nyne,
 haue all commaunded me,
Bycauſe they know, the blynded God
 hath ſome thyng pearced the.
To leade the foorth, a thyng to ſee,
 yf all thyngs happen ryght,
Whiche ſhall gyue the occaſion good,
 with ioyfull mynde to wryght.
To this, I wold haue anſwered ſayne
 and theare began to ſpeake,
But as my words were commyng forth
 my purpoſe he dyd breake.
Come on (quoth he) none Aunſwere now
 we maye no lenger ſtaye.
But frame thy ſelfe, to flye abroade,
 for hence we muſt awaye.
And here withall, on both my ſydes,
 two wyngs me thought dyd growe,
Of mighty breadth, away went he,
 and after hym I flowe.

And euer as we mounted vp,
  I lookte vpon my wyngs,
And prowde I was, me thought to ſee
  ſuche vnacquaynted thyngs.
Tyll foorth we flewe, my Guyde and I,
  with mowntyng flyght apace,
Beholdyng Ryuers, woods, and Hylles
  and many a goodly place.
Till at the length methought I might
  a Gorgyous Caſtell ſpye,
Thear downe began my guyd to fall,
  and downward eake fell I,
Lo heare the place where you muſt light
  Gan *Mercury* to ſaye,
Farwell and note what thou dooſt ſe,
  for I muſt hence away.
And with this ſame a way flewe he,
  and leſte me there alone,
Wher as with Feare a maſde I ſtood,
  and thus began to mone.
Alas where am I now become,
  what Curſed Chaunce hath blown,
Me from the place where I was bred,
  to Countreis heare vnknown,
What ment that fell vnhappy Feend,
  that *Maia* brought to lyght,
To bring me from my Hartes deſyre,
  to ſee thys dolefull ſyght.
Vnhappy Wretche, I wolde I hadde,
  his Perſon heare in hand,
Then ſhuld I wreak mine Ire of him.
  that brought me to this Land.
But all to late alas I wyſh,
  for words auayle not nowe,
Tis beſt to learne. what place it is,
  and yet I knowe not howe.
Alas that here were *Ptholome*,
  with Compaſſe Globe in hande,

Whofe Arte fhuld fhowe me true the place,
  and Clymate where I ftande,
Well yet what foeuer chaunce theron
  what foeuer Realme it be,
Yon Caftell wyll I vyfyte fure,
  hap what hap wyll to me.
Thus much me thought alone I fpoke
  and then I forewarde went,
And curfed eke an hundred folde,
  them that me thyther fent.
Thus to the Caftell, ftrayght I came,
  whiche when I vewde aboute,
And fawe the workmanfhyp therof
  full gorgeouflye fet oute.
I entred in, with fearefull Harte,
  muche doutyng howe to fpeede,
But euer hope of happye chaunce,
  my heauye Hart dyd feede.
Wyde was the Courte and large within
  the walles were rayfed hye,
And all engraued with Storyes fayre
  of coftlye Imagrye.
There myght I fe, with wondrous Arte,
  the Picture porturde playne,
Of olde *Orion* Hunter good,
  whom Scorpions vyle had flayne.
And by hym ftoode his Borfpeare and
  his other Inftruments,
His Net, his Darte, his Courfar, and
  his Hunters reftyng Tents.
And vnder hym was wrytten fayre.
  in Letters all of Golde,
Here lies he flain, with Scorpions fting,
  vnhappy wretche that wolde,
Haue forced the Ladye of this forte
  with ftayne of Royaltie.
To haue confented to his wyll,
  in fylthye Lecherye.

Wherfore beware that enters here,
  what ſoeuer man thou art?
Accounte thy ſelfe but loſt, yf that
  thou bearſte a lecherous Hart.
When I had vewd theſe wrytten lines
  and markde the Storye well,
I ioyed muche, for why I knew,
  Diana there dyd dwell.
Diana ſhe that Goddeſſe is,
  of Virgyns ſacred mynde,
By whom *Orion* Hunter wylde,
  his Fatall ende dyd fynde.
Next vnto hym, I myght beholde,
  Acteon wofull wyght,
In what a manner, all to torne.
  his cruell Dogs hym dyght.
There might be ſeene, theyr gredye mouths
  with Maiſters blud embrued,
And all his owne vnhappye men,
  that faſt theyr Lorde purſued.
And many Storyes more there war
  engraued: to long to tell
What fearefull haps to many men,
  for luſt vncleane befell.
Thus as I ſtoode with muſyng mind
  beholdyng all thyngs theare,
In ruſheth at the Gate behynde
  a Poſt with heauy cheare.
Into the Hall with haſte he hyes
  and after folowed I,
To here what kynde of Newes he brought
  or what he ment therby.
He paſſyng through the Hall in haſte,
  at entraunce neuer ſtayed,
But blowyng faſt for want of breath,
  as one almoſte diſmayed.
Approcht in Preſence to the ſyght
  of chaſte *Dianaes* face,

That all encompaſte rounde aboute
  with Virgyns in that place,
In loftye Chayre of hye eſtate
  dyd ſyt, all clothde in whyte,
Of Syluer hewe, that ſhynyng gaue,
  me thought, a gorgeous ſyght.
There dyd I ſe, fayre *Dido* Queene
  and fayre *Hiſiphile*,
And next to them *Lucretia* ſat,
  and chaſte *Penelope*.
But theſe ſame foure, no Bowes dyd beare
  for Virgyns ſacred ſtate,
They had forſaken long ago,
  and ioynde with faythfull Mate.
On the other ſyde, ſat all the ſorte
  of fayre *Dianaes* trayne,
Whoſe trade with toyle amongſt the woods
  was euer bent to payne.
Whoſe ſacred minds, were ner defyld
  with any wanton luſt,
Whiche neuer could the fyckle ſtate,
  of Louers ſancye truſte.
The chyeſe of them was *Iſmenis*,
  Whom beſt *Diana* loued,
And next in place ſat *Hyale*,
  whom neuer Fancye moued,
Next vnto them ſat *Nipha* ſayre,
  a Gemme of Chaſtyte,
And next to her ſat *Phyale*,
  not baſeſt in degree,
Behynde them all, of paſſyng forme,
  ſayre *Rhanis* held her place,
And nye to her I myght diſcerne
  Dame *Plecas* ſhynyng face,
Theſe Pryncely Nymphes accompanyed
  Diana in her Baynes,
Whyle as in ſhape of Stagge poore wretche
  Acteon had his paynes,

Aboue them all I myght beholde,
as placed before the reſt,
Hipolitus whom *Phedraes* ſpyte?
moſt Cruelly had dreſt.
Hipolitus the vnſpotted Pearle:
of pure Virginitie,
Whoſe noble Hart culd not agre,
to ſtepdames vyllany.
Next vnto hym ſat Continence,
and next was Labour placed?
Of bodie bygge and ſtrong he was,
and ſomwhat Crabtre faced.
Next hym was placed Abſtinence,
a leane vnwyldy wyght,
Whoſe Diet thyn had baniſht cleane,
all fond and vayne delyght.
A Thouſand more me thought ther war
whoſe names I dyd not know,
And yf I did to longe it were,
in Verſes them to ſhow.
Down of his knees the meſſenger
before them al doth fall,
And vnto chaſt *Diana* thear,
for ſuccour thus doth call.
O Goddeſſe chiefe of Chaſtitie,
and Sacred Virgins mynd:
Let Pitie from your noble Hart:
redreſſe for Miſers fynd.
Let not our weryed Hartes ſuſtaine,
ſuche wrongfull Tyranye?
Quench quickly now the fyrie flames
of open Iniurye.
This ſayd for Feare he ſtaied awhyle,
and than began agayne,
A mighty Prynce (quoth he) is com,
with great vnruly trayne.
All armed well at euery poynt.
(a dredefull ſyght to ſe:)

And euery man in feates of armes,
  ryght ſkylfull all they be.
The Captaine chyſe in Charyot ryde
  with pompe and ſtately Pryde :
With Bow in hand of gliſtering gold,
  and Quyuer by his ſyde.
Wher many a ſhaſt full ſharp doth ly:
  and many a mortall Darte,
That hath with poyſoned force deſtroid,
  Full many a yealdyng Harte.
He entred hath within your Realme,
  and taken many a Forte,
Hath ſakte them all, and ſpoylde them quyte
  and ſlayne a wondrous ſorte.
In ſtraungeſt guyſe, for where he ſhoots
  the wounde doth feſter ſtyll
And all the Surgians that we haue
  can not remoue the yll,
In lytell tyme the gryeſe ſo ſore,
  doth growe in euery parte,
Deſtraynyng through the venomed vaines
  doth ſo torment the Hart.
That ſome to ryd them ſelues therof
  in fluds full deepe they leape,
And drown them ſelues ſom downward ſalles
  from Houſes hye by heape,
Some Anker caſt on croſſed Beames
  to ryd them ſelues from ſtryſe,
And hang them ſelues full thycke on trees
  to ende a wretched lyſe.
And they whoſe fearefull mynds dare not
  thus make an ende of wo,
With greuous flames, conſumynge long
  theyr lyſe at length forgo.
Loe here the Somme of all I haue,
  this Tygre vs anoyes,
And cruellye hath ſpoyled vs,
  of all our wonted ioyes.

Whom yf your Grace do not repuls,
and fynde ſome preſent ſtaye,
Vndoubtedly he wyll wyn this Realme,
and take vs all awaye.
At this, the Ladyes all amazde
for feare dyd looke full pale,
And all beheld with mazed eyes,
the Wretche that tolde the tale.
Tyll at the length *Hipolitus*
of Hart and courage hye,
Nothyng abaſhde, with ſodain newes
began thus to replye.
Caſte fere away, faire Dames (quoth he)
diſmaye your ſelues no more,
I know by whom this miſchief ſpryngs
and know a helpe therfore.
It is not ſuche a dredefull Wyght,
as he doth here reporte,
That entred is within theſe partes,
and plagues the ſymple ſorte.
Nor is his force ſo great to feare,
I know it I full well:
It is the ſcornfull blynded Boy,
that neare to vs doth dwell.
Whom *Mars* long tyme a go begott,
of that Laſciuious dame:
That Linckt in Chaines for Lechery,
receaued an open ſhame.
A diſobedient blynded Foole,
that durſt preſume to turne:
His dartes agaynſt his mother ons,
and cauſd her ſore to burne.
An auncient foo: to all this Court,
Of long tyme he hath ben:
And hath attempted euermore,
by this: Renowne to wyn.
His cruell Hart, of Pitie voyed,
doth ſpare no kynd of age:

But tender youth and dotyng age,
he ſtrykes in furyous rage.
And laughes to ſcorne the ſely ſoules
that he hath wounded ſo,
No Fine appoynted of theyr ils,
no end of al theyr wo.
But ſyns he hath preſumed thus,
to entre heare in Place,
And heare to threten Conqueſts thus,
agaynſt *Dianaes* Grace,
Let him be ſure his loſtie Mynde,
this deade ſhall ſoone repent,
If that your grace do here agre,
with Fre and full concent.
To make me Cheſtain of this Charge
and whom I lyſt to choſe,
If Priſoner heare I bryng hym not,
Let me myne Honour loſe.
And there he ceaſde with ioyfull looks
the Ladyes ſmyled all,
And thorough his wordes they hoaped ſoone
to ſe *Cupidoes* fall.
With heauenly voice *Diana* thear,
as chyefe aboue the reſt:
This wiſe her words began to frame,
From out her ſacred breſt.
My good *Hipolitus* quoth ſhe,
whoſe true and faythfull mynd:
In doubtfull daunger often I,
do alwayes redy fynd.
For to reuenge the cankred rage,
of all my ſpytfull foes,
Thou he from whoſe vnſpotted hart,
the fluddes of vertue flowes.
whoſe ſeruiſe long hath ben aproued,
within this court of myne,
Reſtrayne this boyes vnruly rage,
by valyant means of thyne,

I geue the leaue and thee appoint,
  my cheyf Lieutenant here,
Chuſe whom you wilt take whom you lyſt,
  thou nedeſt no whit to feare.
With this he roſe from out his place,
  and lokynge round a bout:
Choſe *Abſtinence* and *Continence*,
  with *Labour* Captayne ſtout.
And with theſe thre he tooke his leaue
  of all the Ladyes there,
Who doubtyng of his ſafe returne,
  let fall full many a teare.
He lefte them theare in heauynes,
  and made no more delaye,
But outward went and toward ye Campe,
  he tooke the neareſt way.
With this the Queenes commyſſion ſtraight
  was ſent abroad in haſte,
To rayſe vp ſouldiars round about,
  and with theyr Captayne plaſte.
To bring them foorth and marching on,
  Hipolitus to meet,
Than ſounded Trumpetes al a broad,
  and Drumes in euery ſtreat.
And ſouldiears good lyke ſwarmes of Bees
  theyr Captains preaſe about
All armed braue in Corſletes white,
  they march with courage ſtout.
And forwarde ſhoue, till at the length
  where as theyr marſhall lyes,
They fynd the place the ioifull ſounds,
  Do mount aboue the ſkyes.
Hipolitus receaued them all,
  with woordes of pleſaunt cheare,
And placith them in good aray,
  bycauſe the camp was neare.
Three Battails big of them he frams,
  and of the Rereward [? Vanguard] ſtrong,

Hath Labour charge who ſteppeth foorth,
before the ſtatlye thronge :
And Captayn of the reare ward next,
was placed abſtinens,
And Ioind to him for Policie,
was Captayne Continence :
The Battayle mayne *Hipolitus*,
him ſelfe did chuſe to guyd.
And in the formeſt front therof,
on Courſer fayre doth ryde :
The *Trumpets* ſound march on apace,
and Dromes the ſame do ſtryke.
Then forward moues ye Army great,
In order Martiall lyke.
I cam behynde (me thought) and beſt,
it ſeamed then to me :
To vew the dynt of dreedfull ſword,
and feyghter none to be.
Thie Spies were ſent abroad to vew,
the place where *Cupide* lay :
A longeſt a Ryuer ſayre and broad,
they ſpye a pleaſaunt way,
Which waye they tooke and paſſynge foorth,
at length apeares a plaine:
Both large and vaſt wher lyes ye rowt,
of Cruell *Cupides* trayne.
Thus told the ſpyes we onward hye,
and ſtrayght in ſyght we haue,
The ferfull ſhow of all our Foes,
and dredfull army braue,
The firſt yat marched from *Cupides* Camp
was drowſy *Idlenes*.
The chyefeſt frend that loue had then,
the next was vyle *Exces*.
A Lubbour great, miſhapen moſt,
of all that thear I ſaw,
As much I thynk in quantitie,
as horſes ſyxe can draw.

A myghty face both broad and flat,
  and all with Rubies set:
Muche nosed lyke a Turky Cocke,
  with teth as blacke as Get.
A Belye byg, full trust with guts,
  and Pestels two, lyke Postes,
A knaue full square in euery poynt,
  A Prynce of dronken Ostes.
Vpon a Camell couched hye,
  for Horse coulde none hym beare,
A mighty Staffe in hande he had,
  his Foes a farre to feare.
Behynde them all, the blynded God,
  doth com in Charyot fayre,
With ragyng flames flong rounde about
  he pestres all the ayre.
And after hym, for tryumphe leades
  a thousande wounded Harts,
That gush abrode hot streams of blud
  new persed with his Dartes,
The army redy for to meete
  and all at poynt to fyght,
Hipolitus with lusty cheare
  and with a noble Spryght.
His Souldiers to encourage. Thus
  his wordes begyns to place.
My valyaunt frends and Subiects all
  of Chast *Dianaes* Grace.
whose noble Harts were neuer staind
  with spot of Dastards mynd,
Behold our enemyes here at hande,
  behold yon coward blynd.
Of lytle force, comparde with you,
  howe in a fond araye,
They stragle out no ordre dewe,
  obserued in theyr waye.
Behold what goodly Guyds they haue
  to gouerne them withall,

That neuer knew what fighting ment
  but lyue to Venus thrall.
Marke hym that guyds the rerewarde there
  that vyle deformed Churle,
Whofe foggy Mates, with paunches fyde
  do thycke aboute him whurle.
And he that formoft hether coms
  loe what a handfome Squyre,
Sure full vnapt to kepe the felde,
  more fyt to fyt by the fyre.
In fyne lo Victorye at hande
  with hye tryumphant Crowne,
Bent for to fpoyle our Foes of Fame,
  and caft theyr Glorye downe.
Fyght therfore now courageouflye,
  and ryd your frendes of feare,
Declare your Manhod valyauntly,
  and let your Harts appeare.
With this the founde begyns to mount
  and noyfe hye to ryfe,
And warlyke tunes begyn to dafh,
  them felues agaynft the Skyes.
The Canons Cracke, begins to roore
  and Darts full thycke they flye
And couerd thycke, the armyes both,
  and framde a Counter Skye.
And now the Battayls both be ioynde
  with ftroke of Hande to trye.
The quarrell iuft and for to fynde,
  where *Victorye* doth lye,
The Souldyers all of *Idlenes*
  where *Labour* coms, do fall,
And wounded fore, by force of hym,
  all bathde in blud, they fprall.
Hym felfe alone with *Idlenes*
  nowe hande to hande doth fyght
And after many a mortall wounde,
  deftroyes the felye wyght.

Then ioynes with him Syr *Abſtinence*
with ayde and ſuccours newe,
And both vpon the greſye Hoaſte,
of Glottonye they ſlewe.
The Captayn doth aduaunce hymſelf
with *Abſtinence* to meete,
The vnweldy Creature ſmitten there
is tombled vnder feete.
Then *Fancie* flyes *Incontinence*
and all *Cupidoes* frendes,
Beholdynge Fortune thus to frowne,
by flyght them ſelfe defendes.
Cupido whan he ſees hymſelfe,
thus ſpoylde of all his ayde,
The chyef Supporters of his Courte,
ſo ſodaynly decayde.
Bad turne his Charyottes than with haſte
and faſt away he flyes,
Amongſt the chaſte *Hipolitus*
on ſwyftye Courſer hyes,
Than all with Ioye they after run,
downe thycke the enemyes fall,
The blinded boy, for ſuccour ſtraight
to *Venus* hye doth call,
But all his cryes auayleth not,
his Foes hym faſt purſewe,
The dryuer of his Charyot ſoone,
Hipolitus there ſlewe.
And down from Horſe, the wretche doth fall.
The horſes ſpoyld of guyde,
A Souldier ſtoute of *Reaſons* bande,
is wylled there to ryde.
Who tur[n]yng Raynes another waye
reſtrayns hym of his flyght,
His Honours loſt and taken thus,
Cupide in dolfull plyght.
Theſe wordes with tremblyng voyce began
ſyth Fortune thus quoth he,

Hath giuen her doome from doubtfull breſt
and turnd her Grace from me.
Syth that the moſt miſſortune nowe,
that euer I could fynd,
Hath chaunced to me and Myſer I,
by Deſtenyes aſſygnde.
Am Captyue heare, conſydre yet,
what Fortune myght haue wrought
And made a Conquerer of me,
and you in Bondage brought.
Conſydre yet the wofull plyght,
wherin you had remaynd,
If that the Gods my happy ſtate,
had not ſo ſore diſdaynd,
And by your Gryef, than meſure mine
ſhowe mercye in this caſe,
That Conquerour commended is,
who gyues to pytie place.
The cruell mynd diſprayſed is,
In euery kynd of ſtate,
No man ſo hauty lyues on earth,
but ons may fynd his mate.
Theſe wordes *Hipolitus* I ſpeake,
to bread no farther ſtryſe,
I ſpeake not this of malyce heare,
my ſute is for my lyſe,
Syth Fortune thus hath fauord you,
graunt this my ſmall requeſt,
And let me lyue yf mercy dwell,
within your Noble breſt,
By this tyme *Morpheus* had diſperſt
the drowſy Clowd of ſleape,
And from my braynes the quyet traunce,
began full faſt to Creape.
And dounward fell. I waked therwith
and lokyng round a bout,
Long tyme I muſed where I was,
my mynd was ſtyl in doubt.

Till at the length I vewde the tree,
and place where as I ſat,
And well beheld the pleaſaunt Spryng
* that late I wondred at.
I ſawe beſyde the Golden Globe,
of *Phebus* ſhynyng bryght,
That Weſtwarde halfe, dyd hyde his face
approchyng faſt the nyght.
Eche Byrde began to ſhrowd hymſelf
in tree to take his reſt
And ceaſte the pleaſaunt tunes yat late
proceaded from theyr Breaſte.
I homewarde went, and left them all,
and reſtles all that nyght,
I muſynge laye, tormented thus,
with fond lamentyng ſpryght.
When *Phebus* roſe to paſſe the tyme,
and paſſe my gryefe awaye
I toke my Pen and pend the Dreame
that made my Muſes ſtaye.

¶ FINIS.

[* This line is repeated. Appearing at the bottom of one page, and also at the top of the next.]

¶ Imprynted at London
in S. Brydes Churchyarde,
by *Thomas Colwell*, for
Raufe Nevvbery.

And are to be sold at his shop
in Fleetestrete, a lytle
aboue the Conduit.

1 5 6 3.

15. *Die Mensis March.*

¶ Faultes escaped in the Pryntynge.

[The whole of these corrections have been embodied in the Text.]

Muir & Paterson, Printers, Edinburgh.

1 OCTOBER 1878.

Please oblige, by showing this List to your friends.

Works in English Literature

PUBLISHED OR TO BE PUBLISHED BY

EDWARD ARBER,

Associate, King's College, London, F.R.G.S., &c.

AT

QUEEN SQUARE, BLOOMSBURY, LONDON, W.C.

Sold by all Booksellers in the United Kingdom, and by the following, abroad:—

erlin: N. ASHER.	Montreal: DAWSON BROTHERS.
ombay: THACKER, VINING & Co.	New York: SCRIBNER, WELFORD & Co.
oston: LITTLE, BROWN & Co.	Philadelphia: C. J. PRICE.
alcutta: THACKER, SPINK & Co.	San Francisco: A. L. BANCROFT & Co.
elbourne: GEORGE ROBERTSON.	Toronto: ADAM, STEVENSON & Co.

*** Foreign booksellers selling these publications can have their names added to e above, in the next List, upon application.

These publications are all edited by Mr. Arber, unless otherwise stated.
Any single work may be obtained separately. In ordering quote the NUMBER, TLE, and PRICE (the author's name is unnecessary).
All orders must be accompanied by a remittance; which, if under 10*s*., can be ade in *Postage Stamps*; if above that sum, in P.O.O., made payable at HIGH OLBORN Office, or Cheques crossed LONDON AND COUNTY BANK.
These publications are ALWAYS on sale; and may be obtained through your own okseller; or, *in any number*, post-free *by return*, on remitting to Mr. ARBER, *the ices*, as stated in this List.
The usual allowance to Colleges and Schools.
All inquiries must be accompanied by a Stamp for reply.
Subscriptions, of not less than One Guinea, can be paid in advance of the appearance of the Publications ordered.

This List cancels all previous ones, as regards Works not yet published.

Richard I.

1196. 1486. *The Revelation to the Monk of Evesham.* . No. 18

Henry VI.—Henry VII.

1422-1509. *The Paston Letters.*

Henry VIII.

1516. 1566. Sir T. MORE. *Utopia.* 14
1527. W. ROY. *Rede me and be nott wrothe.*
1530 [ROY?] *A proper dyaloge betwene a Gentillman, etc.*
1545. R. ASCHAM. *Toxophilus.* 7

Edward VI.

1549. Bp. H. LATIMER. *The Ploughers.* 2
1549. Do. *Seven Sermons before Ed. VI.* 13
1550. Rev. T. LEVER. *Sermon in the Shrouds of St. Pauls.* 25
1550. Do. *Sermon before Ed. VI.* . . 25
1550. Do. *Sermon at Paul's Cross.* . . 25
1553. 1566. N. UDALL. *Roister Doister.* 17
1553. R. EDEN. *Translation from* S. MUNSTER (1532).

Philip and Mary.

1555. R. EDEN. *Translations from* PETER MARTYR (1516), OVIEDO Y VALDES (1521), A. PIGAFETTA (1532), *etc.*
1557. *Tottel's Miscellany. Songes and Sonettes, etc.* . 24

Elizabeth.

1562. 1563. B. GOOGE. *Eglogs, Epytaphes, etc.*
1570. R. ASCHAM. *The Scholemaster.* 23
1575. G. GASCOIGNE. *Notes of Instruction in Eng. verse.* 11
1576. G. GASCOIGNE. *The complaynt of Philomene.* . 11
1576. Do. *The Stele Glasse.* 11
1577. G. WHETSTONE. *A Remembrance of G. Gascoigne.* 11
1579. J. LYLY. *Euphues. The Anatomy of Wit.* . 9
1579. S. GOSSON. *The Schoole of Abuse.* 3
1579. Do. *An Apologie for the School of Abuse.* 3
1580. J. LYLY. *Euphues and his England.* . . . 9
1557-1580. T. TUSSER. *Fiue Hundred Points of Good Husbandrie.*
1582. 1595. Sir P. SIDNEY. *An Apologie for Poetrie.* . . 4
1582. T. WATSON. *The* Ἑκατομπαθία. 21
1583. Rev. P. STUBBES. *The Anatomie of Abuses.*

1589. G. PUTTENHAM. *The Arte of English Poesie.* No. 15
1590. UBALDINI.—RYTHER. *Concerynge the Spanishe fleete.*
1590. T. WATSON. *Melibœus.* 21
1590. Do. *An Eclogue, &c.* 21
1590. E. WEBBE. *His Wonderful Trauailes.* . . 5
1591. Sir W. RALEIGH. *The Fight in the 'Revenge.'*
1592. 1593. T. WATSON. *The Teares of Fancy or Loue disdained.* 21
1593. *The Phœnix Nest.* Ed. by R. S. . . .
1595. G. MARKHAM. *The Tragedie of Sir R. Grenville.*
1597. F. BACON. *Essayes.*

James I.

1604. [JAMES I.] *A Counterblaste to Tobacco.* . . 19
1607-12. Sir *F. Bacon. The Writings, &c. &c.* Harl. MS. 5106.
1612. The *Essaies* of Sir F. BACON, Knt.
? 1653. Sir R. NAUNTON. *Fragmenta Regalia.* . . 20

Charles I.

1625. Francis Lord VERULAM, *Essayes or Counsels.*
1628-33. Bp. J. EARLE. *Microcosmographie.* . . 12
1625-45. 1689. J. SELDEN. *Table Talk.* 6
1634-40. 1640. W. HABINGTON. *Castara.* 22
1637. STAR CHAMBER. *Decree concerning Printing.* 1
1640. F. QUARLES. *Enchyridion.* . . . . .
1641. J. MILTON. *The Reason of Church Government, etc.*
1642. J. HOWELL. *Instructions for Forreine Travell.* 16
1643. LORDS AND COMMONS. *Order regulating of Printing.* 1
1644. J. MILTON. *On Education.*
1644. Do. *Areopagitica.* 1
1645. J. HOWELL. *Epistolæ Ho-Elianæ.* Book I.
1647. J. HOWELL. *Epistolæ Ho-Elianæ.* Book II.

Commonwealth.

1650. J. HOWELL. *Epistolæ Ho-Elianæ.* Book III.
1650. Do. *Instructions for travelling into Turkey.* 16
1655 Do. *Epistolæ Ho-Elianæ.* Book IV.

Charles II.

1671. 1672. G. VILLIERS, Duke of Buckingham, *The Rehearsal.* 10

William and Mary.

1694. E. PHILLIPS. *Life of John Milton.*

SURELY to us, after the Sacred Scriptures, works of devotion and of religious instruction; the Literature of England comes next. However exquisite and subtle the charms of Greek and Grecian literature; however necessary and worthy of study the language and literature of Rome; the writings of our Forefathers come home to every Englishman. What a mighty Literature have we inherited! How little is it known, save to a few, who have devoted all their leisure to its exploration! Authors mighty in Prose and Verse! Writers full of aëry fancies and graceful similitudes! Men whose Prose marches with the tramp and strength of a Roman legion: men whose Song is sung by a Puck or an Ariel; or who sing in it of Patient Grissell, of Fair Geraldine, or of Una and her Red Cross Knight. Above all the English Bible, so clung unto by our ancestors—with its infinite early editions and their most heroic story.

What present nation has so ancient, so vast, so varied a body of writings as England? In which are contained not only the productions of our Arch-Poets, Chaucer, Spenser, Shakespeare, Milton, Dryden; but those of an almost uncountable number of authors, inferior indeed to these, but of high rank among ordinary minds.

Good books, besides affording enjoyment, provoke to like excellence. No man writeth unto himself. Each worthy writer is trained, assimilated, and influenced by those who have gone before: each returning a like benefit to posterity. To trace the continuous chain of influence, of cause and effect, link by link, forms a part of the History of English Literature. That History that we may soon hope to possess, for the first time adequately in our language, in Professor HENRY MORLEY'S work *English Writers*: of which we have already received the earlier instalment, down to Dunbar. What is designed in the *Facsimile Texts*, the *English Reprints*, and the *Annotated Reprints* is to *represent* the later literature by giving, at as cheap a price as can be, Exact Texts sometimes of books already famous, sometimes of those quite forgotten: in some cases, of works that illustrate the Literary History; in other instances, of those that in a sense, constitute it.

The result is already, that these Reproductions are unique in English Bibliography for their accuracy and cheapness, as well as for the unlimited numbers offered constantly for sale: and *so far as they are yet published*, they constitute the best of all introductions to our old Authors, from the time of Caxton to that of Addison. E. A.

P.S.—A word in furtherance of the *Early English Text*, the *Chaucer*, and the *Ballad* Societies. No one knows the extent of the unprinted Literature of England. These Societies are recovering for us book after book; and laying us all under great obligation to their able Editors, who labour gratuitously. For further information, apply to F. J. Furnivall, M.A., 3 St. George's Square, London, N.W.

IN VARYING SIZES, FOLLOWING THE ORIGINALS.

OF European publications there are not a few which the mere outward appearance, their countenance so to speak, possess an extreme interest. Either from the excessive rarity of the book itself, or the drollery or quaintness of its illustrations; either from the literary importance of the work or its significance in the history of our Country or in the progress of the World: there arises at the sight of it the keenest attention, one might almost say an inexpressible sympathy with the book itself. In all such cases: Sun-Portraits confer exquisite and perpetual enjoyment.

Hitherto Cost has debarred photolithographed books from general use; but I trust to offer from time to time, at *ordinary book-prices*, works of this supreme interest, though necessarily of an infinitely diverse character. In which effort, I trust to receive a thorough support from the large number of readers who have sustained the *English Reprints*. Both being like attempts to make forgotten books known; and known books, more perfectly and perpetually obtainable.

Early in November, will be published in Fcp. 4to., Half Calf, Illuminated sides, pp. xxxii.-64.

[WILLIAM TYNDALE, assisted by WILLIAM ROY.

The First *printed* English New Testament. , Cologne—Worms. 1525. 4to.]

Photo-lithographed, by the permission of the Trustees of the British Museum, from the *unique* fragment in the Grenville Collection.

Briefly told, the story of this profoundly interesting work is as follows:—In 1524 TYNDALE went from London to Hamburg; where remaining for about a year, he journeyed on to Cologne: and there assisted by WILLIAM ROY, subsequently the author of the Satire on Wolsey, *Rede me and be nott wrothe* [see p. 11], he began this first edition in 4to; *with glosses* of the English New Testament. A virulent enemy of the Reformation, COCHLÆUS, at that time an exile in Cologne, learnt, through giving wine to the printer's men, that P. Quentel the printer had in hand a secret edition of three thousand copies of the English New Testament. In great alarm, he informed Herman Rinck, Senator of the city, who moved the Senate to stop the printing; but Cochlæus could neither obtain a sight of the Translators, nor a sheet of the impression.

Tyndale and Roy, fled with the printed sheets, up the Rhine to Worms; and there completing this edition, produced also another in Octavo, *without glosses*. Both editions were in England in Jan.-March, 1526: and of the six thousand copies of which they together were composed, there remain but this fragment of the First commenced edition; and of the Second edition, one complete copy in the Library of the Baptist College at Bristol, and an imperfect one in that of St. Paul's Cathedral, London.

The price of this *Facsimile Text*, will be only SIX SHILLINGS.

THE great importance to the increasing study of English Literature, of constantly adding to, and constantly keeping on sale (a more difficult task than at first would appear) at the lowest practicable prices, these Exact Texts; has led to a full consideration of the past three years' progress, in an experiment which has been successful beyond anticipation. The following alterations have been found advisable, in order to place this designedly very cheap Series upon a permanent basis.

The changes to take effect from 1st October 1870.

Small Paper, in Foolscap Octavo.

1. The public choice has passed so generally from *Cut* to *Uncut* edges: that future issues will be in *Uncut* edges only. This will also apply to all reimpressions, as soon as the existing *Cut-edged* copies have been sold.

2. No Sixpenny Reprints will be issued in future. The trouble is out of all proportion to the price.

3. The *maximum* number of pages for Shilling works will be about One hundred and twenty-eight. Experience has proved that number to be the *very utmost* limit practicable for such closely packed works in the costly old spelling, &c.

∴ The result of these changes to the public will be simply, that some future Reprints will be increased in price, by an extra Sixpence. A trifling contribution to enable me to go on for years. Yet I very reluctantly decide on this augmentation: this series being my personal free offering to a more perfect knowledge of English Literature.

All existing issues will be maintained at the present prices.

Large Paper, in Foolscap Quarto.

Nos. 19 to 24 in Large Paper are now ready. A single Large Paper copy can be obtained.

Demy Quarto.

Works in this size will be issued bound in Cloth. When published, copies will however be obtainable in Sheets, for binding, by remitting the price *direct* to me.

There is a great cause for thankfulness in the progress already made. Works which some of our most experienced English scholars never hoped to see reprinted; have been put into *general* circulation. Much more may be accomplished, by a personal advocacy of this Series by *each* Purchaser; with a generous permission to print, from possessors of rare or unique English books; and with unwearying effort on my own part. Maintaining herein the ancient and worthy fame of England; may we lead very many to understand how much pure and unadulterated Delight is to be found in our Old English Authors.

ORDINARY ISSUE IN OCTAVO.

Durable Cases, in Roxburghe style, to hold four or five Reprints. One Shilling each.

BOUND VOLUMES IN OCTAVO.

Two or three of such works, collected into occasional Volumes.

LARGE PAPER EDITION IN QUARTO.

The same texts, beautifully printed on thick toned paper, with ample margins suitable for purposes of study. Issued in Stiff covers, uncut edges. When bound to the purchaser's own taste; these Large Paper Copies form most handsome books.

ANY SINGLE WORK OR VOLUME MAY BE HAD SEPARATELY.

Quarto. *Large Paper Edit.*	FOOLSCAP. *Stiff Covers. Uncut Edges.*	Octavo. *Green Cloth, Red Edges.*
1/6	**1. JOHN MILTON.** (1) A decree of the Starre-Chamber, concerning Printing, made the eleuenth day of July last past. London, 1637. (2) An Order of the Lords and Commons assembled in Parliament for the regulating of Printing, &c. London, 14 June, 1643. (3) *AREOPAGITICA:* A speech of Mr. John Milton for the liberty of Vnlicenc'd Printing, to the Parliament of England. London. [24 November]. 1644. Sixpence.	Vol. I. Milton, Latimer, Gosson. 2/
1/6	**2. HUGH LATIMER,** *Ex-Bishop of Worcester.* *SERMON ON THE PLOUGHERS.* A notable Sermon of ye reuerende father Master Hughe Latimer, whiche he preached in ye Shrouds at paules churche in London, on the xviii daye of Januarye. ¶ The yere of our Loorde MDXLviii. Sixpence.	
1/6	**3. STEPHEN GOSSON,** *Stud. Oxon.* (1) *THE SCHOOLE OF ABUSE.* Conteining a pleasaunt invective against Poets, Pipers, Plaiers, Jesters, and such like Caterpillers of a Commonwealth; Setting up the Flagge of Defiance to their mischievous exercise, and ouerthrowing their Bulwarkes, by Prophane Writers, Naturall reason, and common experience. A discourse as pleasaunt for gentlemen that fauour learning, as profitable for all that wyll follow vertue. London. [August ?] 1579. (2) *AN APOLOGIE OF THE SCHOOLE OF ABUSE,* against Poets, Pipers, and their Excusers. London. [December ?] 1579. Sixpence.	
1/6	**4. SIR PHILIP SYDNEY.** *AN APOLOGIE FOR POETRIE.* Written by the right noble, vertuous and learned Sir Philip Sidney, Knight. London. 1595. Sixpence.	

Quarto. Octavo.

Large Paper Edit. *TITLES, PRICES, etc., etc.* *Stiff Covers. Uncut Edges.* *Green Cloth, Red Edges.*

5. EDWARD WEBBE, *Chief Master Gunner.*

The rare and most vvonderful thinges which Edward Webbe an Englishman borne, hath seene and passed in his troublesome trauailes, in the Citties of Ierusalem, Damasko, Bethelem, and Galely: and in the Landes of Iewrie, Egipt, Grecia, Russia, and in the land of Prester Iohn. Wherein is set foorth his extreame slauerie sustained many yeres togither, in the Gallies and wars of the great Turk against the Landes of Persia, Tartaria, Spaine, and Portugall, with the manner of his releasement, and
1/6 comming into London in May last. London. 1590.
Sixpence.

6. JOHN SELDEN.

TABLE TALK: being the Discourses of John Seldon Esq.; or his Sence of various Matters of Weight and High Consequence relating especially to Religion and
2/6 State. London. 1689. One Shilling.

Vol. II.

Sidney, Webbe, Selden.

2/6

7. ROGER ASCHAM.

TOXOPHILUS. The schole of shooting conteyned in tvvo bookes. To all Gentlemen and yomen of Englande, pleasaunte for theyr pastime to rede, and profitable for theyr use to folow, both in warre and peace. London.
2/6 1545. One Shilling.

8. JOSEPH ADDISON.

CRITICISMS OF MILTON'S PARADISE LOST. From *The Spectator:* being its Saturday issues between
2/6 31 December, 1711, and 3 May, 1712. One Shilling.

Vol. III.

Ascham, Addison.

2/6

9. JOHN LYLY, M.A.

(1) ☾ *EUPHUES. THE ANATOMY OF WIT.* Verie pleasaunt for all Gentlemen to read, and most necessarie to remember. Wherein are contained the delightes that Wit followeth in his youth by the pleasantnesse of loue, and the happinesse he reapeth in age, by the perfectnesse of Wisedome. London. 1579.

(2) ☾ *EUPHUES AND HIS ENGLAND.* Containing his voyage and aduentures, myxed with sundrie pretie discourses of honest Loue, the Description of the Countrey, the Court, and the manners of that Isle. Delightful to be read, and nothing hurtful to be regarded: wher-in there is small offence by lightnesse giuen to the wise, and lesse occasion of loosenes proferred to the wanton. London, 1580. Collated with early subsequent
9/ editions. Four Shillings.

Vol. IV.

Lyly.

5/

Quarto. | *Large Paper Edit.* — *TITLES, PRICES, etc., etc.* — *Stiff Covers. Uncut Edges.* | Octavo. *Green Cloth, Red Edges.*

10. GEORGE VILLIERS, *Duke of Buckingham.*

THE REHEARSAL. As it was acted at the Theatre Royal London, 1672. With Illustrations from previous
2/6 plays, &c. One Shilling.

11. GEORGE GASCOIGNE, *Esquire.*

(1) A remembravnce of the wel imployed life, and godly end of George Gaskoigne, Esquire, who deceassed at Stalmford in Lincoln shire, the 7 of October 1577. The reporte of GEOR WHETSTONS, Gent an eye witness of his Godly and Charitable End in this world. Lond. 1577.

(2) Certayne notes of Instruction concerning the making of verse or rime in English, vvritten at the request of Master *Edouardi Donati.* 1575.

(3) *THE STEELE GLAS.* A Satyre compiled by George Gasscoigne Esquire [Written between Apr. 1575 & Apr. 1576]. Together with

(4) *THE COMPLAYNT OF PHYLOMENE.* An Elegie compyled by George Gasscoigne Esquire [between
2/6 April 1562 and 3rd April 1575.] London. 1576.
One Shilling.

12. JOHN EARLE, M.A.: *afterwards in succession Bishop of Worcester, and of Salisbury.*

MICRO-COSMOGRAPHIE, or a Peece of the World discovered, in Essays and Characters. London. 1628. With the additions in subsequent editions during the
2/6 Author's life time. One Shilling.

Vol. V. — Villiers, Gascoigne, Earle. 3/6

13. HUGH LATIMER, *Ex-Bishop of Worcester.*

SEVEN SERMONS BEFORE EDWARD VI.

(1) ¶ The fyrste sermon of Mayster Hugh Latimer, whiche he preached before the Kynges Maiest. wythin his graces palayce at Westmynster. M.D.XLIX. the viii of Marche. (,‘,)

(2) The seconde [to seventh] Sermon of Master Hughe Latimer, whych he preached before the Kynges maiestie, withyn hys graces Palayce at Westminster ye. xv. day of
4/ March. M.cccc.xlix. Eighteen Pence.

14. SIR THOMAS MORE.

UTOPIA. A frutefull pleasaunt, and wittie worke, of the best state of a publique weale, and of the new yle, called Utopia: written in Latine, by the right worthie and famous Sir Thomas More knyght, and translated into Englishe by RAPHE ROBYNSON, sometime fellowe of Corpus Christi College in Oxford, and nowe by him at this seconde edition newlie perused and corrected, and also with diuers notes in the margent augmented. London.
2/6 [1556]. One Shilling.

Vol. VI. — Latimer, More. 3/

Quarto. *Large Paper Edit.*	*TITLES, PRICES, etc., etc.* *Stiff Covers. Uncut Edges.*	Octavo. *Green Cloth, Red Edges.*
5/	**15. GEORGE PUTTENHAM.** *THE ARTE OF ENGLISH POESIE.* Contriued into three Bookes: The first of Poets and Poesie, the second of Proportion, the third of Ornament. London. 1589. Two Shillings.	Vol. VII. Puttenham. 2/6
1/6	**16. JAMES HOWELL,** *Historiographer Royal to Charles II.* *INSTRUCTIONS FOR FORREINE TRAVELL.* Shewing by what *cours*, and in what *compasse of time*, one may take an exact Survey of the Kingdomes and States of Christendome, and arriue to the practicall knowledge of the Languages, to good purpose. London. 1642. Collated with the edition of 1656; and in its 'new Appendix for Travelling into *Turkey* and the *Levant* parts' added. Sixpence.	Vol. VIII.
1/6	**17. The earliest known English comedy. NICHOLAS UDALL,** *Master of Eton.* *ROISTER DOISTER,* [from the unique copy at Eton College]. 1566. Sixpence.	Howell, Udall,
2/6	18. *THE REVELATION TO THE MONK OF EVESHAM.* Here begynnyth a marvelous revelacion that was schewyd of almighty god by sent Nycholas to a monke of Euyshamme yn the days of Kynge Richard the fyrst. And the yere of our lord. M.C.Lxxxxvi. [From the unique copy, printed abont 1482, in the British Museum]. One Shilling.	Monk of Evesham JamesVI. 3/6
2/6	**19. JAMES VI.** *of Scotland,* **I.** *of England.* (1) *THE ESSAYES OF A PRENTISE, IN THE DIVINE ART OF POESIE.* Edinburgh 1585. (2) *A COUNTER BLASTE TO TOBACCO.* London. 1604. One Shilling.	
1/6	**20. SIR ROBERT NAUNTON,** *Master of the Court of Wards.* *FRAGMENTA REGALIA:* or, Observations on the late Queen Elizabeth, her Times, and Favourites. [Third Edition. London] 1653. Sixpence.	Vol. IX.
	21. THOMAS WATSON, *Student at law.* (1) *THE* Ἑκατομπαθία or Passionate Centurie of Loue. *Divided into two parts: whereof, the first expresseth the Authors sufferance in Loue: the latter, his long farewell to Loue and all his tyrannie.* Composed by *Thomas Watson* Gentleman; and published at the request of certaine Gentlemen his very frendes. London [1582.]	Naunton, Watson. 2/6

uarto. rge aper dit.	*TITLES, PRICES, etc., etc.* *Stiff Covers. Uncut Edges.*	Octavo. *Green Cloth, Red Edges.*
	(2) *MELIBŒUS* T. Watsoni, Ecloga in obitum F. Walsinghami, &c. Londini, 1590.	
	(3) *AN EGLOGUE*, &c., Written first in latine [the above MELIBŒUS] by *Thomas Watson* Gentleman and now by himselfe translated into English. London 1590.	
4/	(4) *THE TEARS OF FANCY*, or Loue disdained. [From the unique copy, wanting Sonnets ix.-xvi., in the possession of S. Christie-Miller, Esq.] London, 1593. Eighteen Pence.	
2/6	**22. WILLIAM HABINGTON.** *CASTARA.* The third Edition. Corrected and augmented. London. 1640. With the variations of the two previous editions. One Shilling.	Vol. X. Habington, Ascham. 2/6
2/6	**23. ROGER ASCHAM.** *THE SCHOLEMASTER*, Or plaine and perfite way of teachyng children, to vnderstand, write, and speake, the Latin tong, but specially purposed for the priuate brynging vp of youth in Ientlemen and Noble mens houses, commodious also for all such, as haue forgot the Latin tongue, and would, by themselues, without a Scholemaster, in short tyme, and with small paines, recouer a sufficient habilitie, to vnderstand, write, and speake Latin. London. 1570. One Shilling.	
3/6	**24. Tottel's Miscellany.** *SONGES AND SONETTES*, written by the ryght honorable Lorde HENRY HAWARD, late Erle of Surrey, and other. [London, 5 June] 1557. Half-a-crown.	Vol. XI. Tottel. 3/
4/	**25. REV. THOMAS LEVER, M.A.:** *afterwards Master of St John's College, Cambridge.* *SERMONS.* (1) A fruitfull Sermon made in Paules churche at London in the Shroudes, the second of Februari. 1550. (2) A Sermon preached the thyrd [or fourth] Sunday in Lent before the Kynges Maiestie, and his honourable counsell. 1550. (3) A Sermon preached at Pauls Crosse, the xiiii. day of December 1550. Eighteen Pence.	Vol. XII. Lever, Webbe. 3/
2/6	**26. WILLIAM WEBBE,** *Graduate.* *A DISCOURSE OF ENGLISH POETRIE.* Together, with the Authors iudgment, touching the reformation of our English Verse. London. 1586. One Shilling.	

∴ *The following works are designed for publication in time to come. Their prices cannot be fixed with precision, but are approximately given.* Ferrex and Porrex *has been postponed; and*

Newes from the North by F. T. [FRANCIS THYNNE], *with* RICHARD BARNFIELD'S Poems *have not been inserted; some of the Texts not being accessible, at the present time.* J. HOWELL'S Epistolæ Ho-Elianæ *will be put to press as soon as No.* 27 BACON'S Essayes, &c., *is finished.*

Large Paper Edit.		*Stiff Covers. Uncut Edges.*	*Green Cloth, Red Edges.*
7/6	**27. FRANCIS BACON.** A harmony of the *ESSAYES*, &c. The four principle texts appearing in parallel columns.; (1) Essayes. Religious Meditations. Places of perswasion and disswasion. London 1597. (10 Essays.) Of the Coulers of good and euill a fragment. 1597. (2) The writings of Sir Francis Bacon Knt: the Kinges Sollicitor Generall: in Moralitie, Policie, and Historie. *Harleian MS.* 5106. Transcribed bet. 1607-12. (34 Essays.) (3) THE ESSAIES of Sir FRANCIS BACON Knight, the Kings Sollicitor Generall. London 1612. (38 Essays.) (4) The Essayes or Counsels, Ciuill and Morall, of FRANCIS LO. VERULAM Viscount ST. ALBANS. *Newly Written.* 1626. (58 Essays.)	Three Shillings.	Vol. XIII. Bacon. 3/6
2/6	**28. WILLIAM ROY,** *Franciscan Friar.* (1) *REDE ME AND BE NOTT WROTHE.* [Strasburg. 1527. This is his famous Satire on Wolsey.] (2) *A PROPER DYALOGE BETWEEN A GENTLEMAN AND A HUSBANDMAN, &c.* [Attributed to Roy] Marburg. 1530.	Eighteen Pence.	Vol. XIV. Roy, Fight in the Revenge. Googe. 4/
2/6	**29. SIR W. RALEIGH—G. MARKHAM.** *THE LAST FIGHT OF THE REVENGE AT SEA.* (1) A report of the Truth of the fight about the Isles of Acores, this last Sommer. Betvvixt the Reuenge, one of her Maiesties Shippes, and an Armada of the King of Spaine. By Sir Walter Raleigh. London. 1591. (2) The most Honorable Tragedie of Sir Richarde Grinuille, Knight (.·.) *Bramo assai, poco spero, nulla chieggio.* [By GERVASE MARKHAM] London. 1595. [Two copies only are known, Mr. Grenville's cost £40.]	One Shilling.	
2/6	**30. BARNABE GOOGE.** *EGLOGS, EPYTAPHES AND SONETTES* newly written by Barnabe Googe. London 1563. 15 March.	One Shilling.	
	31. REV. PHILLIP STUBBES. (1) *THE ANATOMIE OF ABUSES:* conteyning a discoverie or briefe Summarie of Such Notable Vices and Imperfections, as now raigne in many Christian		

Quarto. Octavo.

Large Paper Edit. — *TITLES, PRICES, etc., etc.* *Stiff Covers. Uncut Edges.* — *Green Cloth Red Edges*

Countreyes of the World : but especialie in a very famous
ILANDE called AILGNA [*i.e.* Anglia] : Together with Vol.
most fearefull Examples of Gods Iudgementes, executed
vpon the wicked for the same, aswell in AILGNA of late,
as in other places, elsewhere. . . London. 1 Maij. 1583. Stubbes.
(2) The Second part of *THE ANATOMIE OF*
6/6 *ABUSES.* . . . London. 1583. Half-a-crown. 3/

32. THOMAS TUSSER.

FIVE HUNDRED POINTES OF GOOD HUSBANDRIE, as well for the Champion, or open Countrie, as also for the woodland, or Seuerall, mixed in euery Month with *HUSWIFERIE*, ... with diuers other lessons, as a diet for the former, of the properties
of windes, plantes, hops, herbes, bees and approued re- Vol.
medies for sheepe and cattle, with many other matters
both profitable and not vnpleasant for the Reader . .
4/ . . London. 1580. Eighteen Pence. Tusser,

33. JOHN MILTON.

Milton.

(1) The Life of Mr John Milton [by his nephew EDWARD PHILLIPS]. From '*Letters of State written by Mr. John Milton*, bet. 1649-59.' London. 1694. 3/
(2) *THE REASON OF CHURCH GOVERNEMENT* urg'd against Prelacy. By Mr. *John Milton*. In two Books. [London] 1641.
(3) Milton's Letter *OF EDUCATION*. To Master
2/6 *Samuel Hartlib.* [London. 5 June 1644.]
One Shilling.

34. FRANCIS QUARLES.

ENCHYRIDION, containing

Institutions — Divine { *Contemplative.* *Practicall.* } — Morall { *Ethycall.* *Oeconomicall.* *Politicall.* } London. 1640-1. Vol.

2/6 One Shilling. Quarles.

35. The Sixth English Poetical Miscellany.

THE PHOENIX NEST. Built vp with the most rare and refined workes of Noble men, woorthy Knights, gallant Gentlemen, Masters of Arts, and braue Schoolers. Full of varietie, excellent inuention, and singular delight. *Never before this time published.* Set forth by R. S. of the
2/6 Inner Temple Gentleman. London 1593. One Shilling. The Phoenix Nest. 2/6

36. SIR THOMAS ELYOT.

Vol.

THE GOVERNOR. The boke named the Gouernor, deuised by ye Thomas Elyot Knight. Londini M.D.xxxi. Elyot.
6/6 Collated with subsequent editions. Half-a-crown. 3/

Demy Quarto.

Will be ready, about March 1871, *in one Volume*, 12*s*. 6*d*.

801. RICHARD EDEN.

I. A treatyse *OF THE NEWE INDIA, WITH OTHER NEW FOUNDE LANDES AND ISLANDS, ASWELL EASTWARDE AS WESTWARDE*, as they are knowen and found in these oure dayes, after the descripcion of SEBASTIAN MUNSTER, in his boke of vniuersall Cosmographie, &c. [London, 1553.]

II. **The First English Collection of Voyages, Traffics, and Discoveries.**— *THE DECADES OF THE NEW WORLD OR WEST INDIA, &c. &c.* [by Peter Martyr of Angleria.] [Translated, compiled, &c. by Richard Eden.] Londini, Anno 1555.

1. The [Dedicatory] Epistle [to King Philip and Queen Mary.]
2. Richard Eden to the Reader.
3. The [1st, 2nd, and 3d only of the 8] Decades of the newe worlde or west India, Conteynyng the nauigations and conquestes of the Spanyardes, with the particular description of the moste ryche and large lands and Ilandes lately founde in the west Ocean perteynyng to the inheritance of the kinges of Spayne. In the which the diligent reader may not only consyder what commoditie may hereby chaunce to the hole christian world in tyme to come, but also learne many secreates touchynge the lande, the sea, and the starres, very necessarie to be knowen to al such as shal attempte any nauigations, or otherwise haue delite to beholde the strange and woonderful woorkes of god and nature. Wrytten in the Latine tounge by PETER MARTYR of Angleria, and translated into Englysshe by RYCHARDE EDEN.
4. The Bull of Pope Alexander VI. in 1493, granting to the Spaniards 'the Regions and Ilandes founde in the Weste Ocean' by them.
5. *The Historie of the West Indies* by GONÇALO FERNANDEZ OVIEDO Y VALDES.
6. Of other notable things gathered out of dyuers autors.
7. Of Moscouie and Cathay.
8. Other notable thynges as touchynge the Indies [chiefly out of the bookes of FRANCISCO LOPEZ DE GOMARA, 'and partly also out of the caade made by SEBASTIAN CABOT.']
9. The Booke of Metals.
10. The description of the two viages made owt of England into Guinea in Affricke [1553, 1554].
11. The maner of fyndynge the Longitude of regions.

INDEX.

∴ An abridged analysis of this voluminous work was issued in the previous catalogue (1 Dec. 1869); which will be found bound up with 'English Reprints' issued during this year, 1870.

Imperial Folio.

1001. PETRUCCIO UBALDINI—AUGUSTINI RYTHER.

A Discourse concerning the Spanishe fleete inuading Englande in the yeare 1588 and ouerthrowne by her Maie: ties Nauie vnder the conduction of the Right-honorable th Lorde Charles Howarde highe Admirall of Englande written in Italian by PETRUCCIO VBALDINI citizen of Flo ence, and translated for A. RYTHER: vnto the which discours are annexed certain tables expressinge the generall exploite and conflictes had with the said fleete.

These bookes with the tables belonginge to them are t be solde at the shoppe of A. RYTHER, being a little fro Leaden hall next to the Signe of the Tower. [1590.]

The twelve Tables express the following subjects :—

FRONTISPIECE.

I. THE SPANISH ARMADA COMING INTO THE CHANNEL, OPPOSIT THE LIZARD; AS IT WAS FIRST DISCOVERED.

II. THE SPANISH ARMADA AGAINST FOWEY, DRAWN UP IN TI FORM OF A HALF MOON; THE ENGLISH FLEET PURSUING.

III. THE FIRST ENGAGEMENT BETWEEN THE TWO FLEET AFTER WHICH THE ENGLISH GIVE CHASE TO THE SPANIARDS, WI DRAW THEIR SHIPS INTO A BALL.

IV. DE VALDEZ'S GALLEON SPRINGS HER FOREMAST, AND IS TAKE BY SIR FRANCIS DRAKE. THE LORD ADMIRAL WITH THE 'BEA AND THE 'MARY ROSE,' PURSUE THE ENEMY, WHO SAIL IN TI FORM OF A HALF MOON.

V. THE ADMIRAL'S SHIP OF THE GUIPUSCOAN SQUADRON HAVIN CAUGHT FIRE, IS TAKEN BY THE ENGLISH. THE ARMADA CO TINUES ITS COURSE, IN A HALF MOON; UNTIL OFF THE ISLE C PORTLAND, WHERE ENSUES THE SECOND ENGAGEMENT.

VI. SOME ENGLISH SHIPS ATTACK THE SPANIARDS TO THE WES WARD. THE ARMADA AGAIN DRAWING INTO A BALL, KEEPS ON I COURSE FOLLOWED BY THE ENGLISH.

VII. THE THIRD AND THE SHARPEST FIGHT BETWEEN THE TV FLEETS: OFF THE ISLE OF WIGHT.

VIII. THE ARMADA SAILING UP CHANNEL TOWARDS CALAIS; TI ENGLISH FLEET FOLLOWING CLOSE.

IX. THE SPANIARDS AT ANCHOR OFF CALAIS. THE FIRESHI APPROACHING. THE ENGLISH PREPARING TO PURSUE.

X. THE FINAL BATTLE. THE ARMADA FLYING TO THE NORT WARD. THE CHIEF GALLEASS STRANDED NEAR CALAIS.

LARGE MAP SHOWING THE TRACK OF THE ARMADA ROUND THE BRITISH ISLES.

These plates, which are a most valuable and early representation of the Spani Invasion, are being re-engraved in *facsimile*, and will be issued in the Spring of 18; at the lowest feasible price: probably HALF-A-GUINEA.

∴ *Other works may follow.*

BY VARIOUS EDITORS: UNDER MR. ARBER'S GENERAL SUPERVISION.

Some Texts require the amplest elucidation and illustration by Masters in special departments of knowledge. To recover and perpetuate such Works is to render the greatest service to Learning. With the aid of Scholars in special subjects, I hope to endow our readers with some knowledge of the Past, that is now quite out of their reach. While the Editors will be responsible both for Text and Illustrations; the works will be produced under my general oversight: so that the Annotated Reprints, *though of much slower growth, will more than equal in value the* English Reprints. E. A.

In the Spring of 1871: in Fcp. 8vo the First Volume (to be completed in Four) of

The Paston Letters. 1422-1509.

Edited by JAMES GAIRDNER, Esq., of the Public Record Office.

EVERY one knows what a blank is the history of England during the Wars of of the two Roses. Amid the civil commotions, literature almost died out. The principal poetry of the period is that of Lydgate, the Monk of Bury. The prose is still more scanty. The monastic Chronicles are far less numerous than at earlier periods: and by the end of the Fifteenth Century they seem to have entirely ceased. Thus it has come to pass that less is known of this age than of any other in our history. In this general dearth of information recent historians like Lingard, Turner, Pauli, and Knight, who have treated of the reigns of Henry VI., Edward IV., &c., have found in *The Paston Letters* not only unrivalled illustration of the Social Life of England, but also most important information, at first hand, as to the Political Events of that time. So that the printed Correspondence is cited page after page in their several histories of this period.

The Paston Letters have not however been half published. No literary use was made of them while accumulating in the family muniment room. William, 2nd Earl of Yarmouth, the last member of the family, having encumbered his inheritance, parted with all his property. The family letters came about 1728 into the hands of the distinguished antiquary, Peter le Neve; afterwards, by his marriage to Le Neve's widow, to his brother antiquary Martin of Palgrave; on his death again, to a Mr. Worth, from whom they were acquired by Mr. afterwards Sir John Fenn.

In 1787, Fenn published a small selection of the Letters in two volumes 4to; of which the first edition having been sold off in a week, a second appeared in the course of the year. He then prepared a further selection, of which two volumes appeared in 1789; the fifth volume being published after his death, in 1823.

Strangely enough, the Original Letters disappeared soon after their publication: and only those of the Fifth volume have, as yet, been recovered. There is no reasonable doubt that they still exist and will some day be found. There is no necessity, however, to postpone a new edition indefinitely, until they are again brought to light: for a comparison of the Fifth volume with its originals establishes Sir John Fenn's general faithfulness as to the Text; and therefore our present possession, in his Edition, of the contents of the missing Manuscripts.

Three hundred and eighty-seven letters in all were published by Fenn: about Four hundred additional letters or documents, belonging to the same collection and which have never been published at all, will be included in the present edition.

Not only will the Text be doubled in quantity; but in its elucidation, it will have the benefit of Mr. Gairdner's concentrated study of this Correspondence for years past. Half his difficulty will be in the unravelling of the chronology of the Letters, partly from internal evidence, partly from the Public Records, and other sources. Fenn's chronology—for no fault of his—is excessively misleading. This was inevitable, from the difficulties of a first attempt, the state of historic criticism in his day, and the limited means then available for consulting the public records, &c. It is hoped, however, by restoring each Letter to its certain or approximate date, vastly to increase the interest of this Correspondence. In addition textual difficulties will be removed, and valuable biographical information afforded.

The Letters of the reign of Henry VI. will form Vol. I. (estimated at about 600 *pp.*): those of Edward IV., Vols. II. and III. (together about 800 *pp.*); and those of Richard III. and Henry VII., Vol. IV. (about 300 *pp.*). The price will be *about* one shilling for every 100 *pp.*; and the work, it is expected, will be completed in Two years.

CPSIA information can be obtained
at www.ICGtesting.com
Printed in the USA
LVHW100612210323
742065LV00002B/261

9 783382 126612